"Dionne, can't you tell when a man is attracted to you?"

She felt Nick's heat searing her through her clothing, even though their bodies weren't touching. Her hands were spread out against his chest to hold him away from her, but they were a feeble defense.

"You aren't attracted to me, Nick. You're curious about the girl who left town under mysterious circumstances. You can't understand why she'd leave a life of luxury behind, can't stand not knowing where she's been or what's she been doing. It's a puzzle, and you're intrigued by puzzles until they're solved. Well, my life is not a game of twenty questions."

Relaxing his grip but not releasing her, Nick murmured, "You're partly right. I am curious about why you left and where you've been." He raised a hand to her face. "But it's you who interests me, not who your father was." His thumb brushed the streak of dirt on her cheek, then caressed her full bottom lip. He watched her eyes widen in reaction. "You feel this, too, Dionne. I've never experienced anything like this. I don't go around wanting to tear a woman's clothes off the moment I see her."

"I didn't come back to get involved with you, Nick. I don't need any complications," Dionne said, trying to appear calm.

"Well, you've got one. . . ."

WHAT ARE *LOVESWEPT* ROMANCES?

They are stories of true romance and touching emotion. We believe those two very important ingredients are constants in our highly sensual and very believable stories in the *LOVESWEPT* line. Our goal is to give you, the reader, stories of consistently high quality that may sometimes make you laugh, sometimes make you cry, but are always fresh and creative and contain many delightful surprises within their pages.

Most romance fans read an enormous number of books. Those they truly love, they keep. Others may be traded with friends and soon forgotten. We hope that each *LOVESWEPT* romance will be a treasure—a "keeper." We will always try to publish

LOVE STORIES YOU'LL NEVER FORGET
BY AUTHORS YOU'LL ALWAYS REMEMBER

The Editors

LOVESWEPT® • 415

Patt Bucheister
Relentless

BANTAM BOOKS
NEW YORK • TORONTO • LONDON • SYDNEY • AUCKLAND

RELENTLESS

A Bantam Book / August 1990

If you would be interested in receiving protective vinyl
covers for your Loveswept books, please write to this address
for information:

Loveswept
Bantam Books
P.O. Box 985
Hicksville, NY 11802

ISBN 0-553-44045-4

Published simultaneously in the United States and Canada

PRINTED IN THE UNITED STATES OF AMERICA

OPM   0 9 8 7 6 5 4 3 2 1

One

If there was one thing Nick Lyon hated, it was waste. So far he'd already wasted fifteen minutes. But waste was why he was there waiting to meet with Dionne Hart, and he'd stick it out.

As he glanced around the lobby of the Hart Corporation offices, the young receptionist raised her hand to her complicated hairstyle, patting any stray tendril that might have escaped the carpet of hair spray. Nick could have told her it would be impossible for anything short of an earthquake to unsettle her hair. He returned her smile, although without the blatant invitation shaping her mouth.

He was always amused when women reacted to him as the redhead had. He never thought much about the reasons for their attraction to him, though he admitted he took full advantage of it

when he was in the mood for female companion-
ship. The face that looked back at him when he
shaved every morning seemed unremarkable to
him. His hair was thick and straight, a little
longer than fashionable, but only because he
usually forgot to get it trimmed regularly. His
tall, lean frame, high cheekbones, dark brown hair
and eyes, and aquiline nose were due to genetics,
and he took them for granted. He preferred to
judge people on more than their appearance, and
often wished everybody felt the same way.

Still, women had always come easily to him.
Too easily, according to his friend Marty Lawson.
Marty had once told him that one of the reasons
women were so attracted to Nick was because
although he enjoyed their company, he also liked
being alone. A prize was worth more if you had to
work for it.

Marty had gone on to predict that one day Nick
would meet a woman who didn't immediately fall
at his feet. For once he would have to work at
getting a woman, and Marty just hoped to see it.
Nick had laughed, not bothering to argue. Marty
could believe whatever he wanted. Nick was comfortable with his life the way it was. If he occasionally felt something was missing, he put it down to
boredom and worked at alleviating the momen-
tary restlessness.

But boredom was certainly not what he was
feeling right then, he thought, shifting in his
chair, which felt like it was padded with concrete. There was nothing lightweight about the

Hart offices. From the moment he had stepped into the building, he had been met with formality of one sort or another, from the dark gray marble floors and walls to the sober-faced personnel. The Titian-haired receptionist who kept giving him provocative glances was the only exception he had seen so far. The color scheme of gray carpets and maroon-trimmed gray walls was oppressive rather than impressive, the decor more in keeping with a mausoleum than a corporate headquarters.

He wanted to blame the heavy atmosphere for the edgy feeling that had crept up on him since he'd gotten there. He couldn't remember the last time he'd had a case of nerves. As an experienced journalist, he thought there was little that could surprise him anymore. Apparently he was wrong. He should only be experiencing curiosity, not this strange anticipation.

Curiosity was one of the traits that made him a good journalist. It was also one of the reasons he was waiting to see Dionne Hart. He wanted to see how the years had changed her, whether she had become as cold and calculating as her father. And he wanted to find out if years ago he had hurt her as much as he suspected he had.

The last time he had seen her, she had been painfully embarrassed at his turning down her invitation to her sixteenth birthday party. Since he was two years ahead of her in school, he'd rarely paid much attention to her, concentrating instead on sports and the numerous uncomplicated girls who flocked around him. He could only guess at how much courage it had taken for Dionne to ask him to her party.

Her shy invitation had taken him completely by surprise, which partially accounted for his blunt negative reply, tactlessly blurted out. He could still remember the stricken look in her eyes.

Those deep blue eyes of hers had stayed with him over the past fourteen years, and he thought about them at odd times without understanding why. They had been the most expressive, haunted eyes he had ever seen, then or now. He remembered the day, several months before her sixteenth birthday, when he had arrived home to find her in the kitchen with his mother. After his father had died when he was six, his mother had gone to work as a cook for Dionne's father, Farrell Hart. Over the years Hart's guests had called her to cook for special occasions, and when he was fifteen she had started her own catering business. She had stayed in touch with Dionne, though.

The moment Dionne had looked up and seen him standing in the kitchen doorway, embarrassment and a strange sadness had darkened her beautiful eyes. She made her excuses and left in the limousine that had been parked in the driveway of their small tract home. When he had asked his mother why Dionne had been there, Blanche Lyon had only shaken her head and refused to comment.

Later he had heard that Dionne's birthday party had never taken place. With the arrogance of youth, he'd wondered if his turning down her invitation was the reason she had canceled it. His mother had been hired to cater the party, and several days later she received a check in the mail for her full fee. Blanche had slowly torn up the check, letting it fall into a wastebasket.

A few weeks after that, Dionne had left school in the middle of the year. No one knew why she had left or where she had gone. A glut of rumors had circulated around school, suggesting Dionne was pregnant, or had contracted a horrible, disfiguring disease and been placed in some sort of institution. It was the first time in Nick's memory that Farrell Hart remained silent with the press, giving no clues to his daughter's whereabouts.

Now Dionne was back.

Nick's hand automatically dipped into his shirt pocket, but found it empty. His mouth twisted, and he dropped his hand. He had heard several people say they'd never craved a cigarette after they quit smoking. They lied. He had quit six months ago, and there were still times when he would have given the title to his classic Mustang for a cigarette. Like now.

Responding to a brief buzzing sound from her phone, the receptionist pushed back her chair and stepped over to the door that led to the executive offices. "Miss Hart will see you now, Mr. Lyon."

She watched him walk toward the door, her gaze slowly sliding from his face to his hips. Nick's stride didn't falter. Stopping near the door, he waited for her to move out of his way. She didn't, and he recognized the bold invitation in her eyes.

Moving her hand off the doorknob, he smiled crookedly. "Maybe some other time."

He strode into the inner office where a dignified older woman sat rigidly behind a desk, like a plump statue draped in gray polyester. She repeated exactly what the receptionist had said, but without the warm smile, and indicated a set of double doors with an imperious wave of her hand. Also, unlike the receptionist, she didn't appear at all interested in the way he walked.

Placing his hands on the double latches, he paused for a moment, then opened the doors.

In the middle of the room, two maroon leather sofas faced each other on either side of a massive Oriental carpet, creating a path for people to follow leading directly to the imposing mahogany desk at the far end of the room. He briefly noticed the few large plants and the contemporary splashes of paint on canvas adorning the walls. Then all his attention centered on the woman sitting behind the desk.

Her head was bent as she wrote on the pad of paper in front of her, holding the pen in her left hand. Her honey-blond hair was pulled into a severe, neat knot behind her head. When she looked up, he was disappointed that the oversized glasses perched on her petite nose partially hid her eyes. This was not the blushing teenager, he thought, who had worn shapeless sweaters and baggy skirts and turned red every time he looked at her. This was a sophisticated, mature woman. Her gaze flowed over him, taking in his black slacks, ivory shirt, and dark gray jacket before returning to his face.

Nick felt the impact of her gaze like a punch in the stomach, and he couldn't look away. The receptionist had practically eaten him with her eyes, and he had felt nothing but amusement. Dionne's glance barely brushed over him, and his body reacted as though she had touched him intimately. A strange pressure built in his chest, until he realized he had been holding his breath since he'd entered the room.

Exhaling, he closed the doors and leaned against them. "Hello, Dionne."

She lifted a brow, her only indication of surprise at his use of her first name. "Mr. Lyon," she said formally, pushing her chair back and standing up. Coming around the desk, she gestured toward one of the sofas. "Won't you be seated?"

Dressed in a light tan suit and white silk blouse, she looked elegant, sophisticated—and untouchable. He couldn't see anything of the fifteen-year-old he had known. This woman bore no resemblance to that shy girl. What had he expected? he asked himself with wry amusement. That she would duck under the desk as soon as he came into the room?

Nick pushed away from the doors and walked slowly toward her. Ignoring her invitation to sit, he stopped a couple of feet away from her. "I was hoping you would remember me, Dionne. It would make what I have to ask you a little easier."

She removed her glasses and set them on the

desk behind her. "I know who you are, Mr. Lyon. I've read your weekly column, 'The Lyon's Roar.' "

That wasn't what he meant, and he had the feeling she knew it. Her answer didn't help him figure out where she had been living, either, since his column appeared in newspapers all over the country.

"This might sound like a line," he said, "but I'll chance it since it's true. We went to school together. I admit it was a long time ago, but I remember you."

She smiled faintly, then walked past him and sat down on one of the sofas. "If you've come to invite me to a class reunion, I'm afraid I don't qualify. I didn't finish school at Monterey High." Gesturing toward the sofa opposite her, she added, "Please sit down, Mr. Lyon. I'll get a crink in my neck if I have to keep looking up at you. Would you care for some coffee?"

Bemused, he sat down on the plush sofa. "No, thank you," he murmured. For a moment he simply stared at her. Though her dark blue eyes were exactly as he remembered them, this meeting wasn't going at all the way he thought it would.

Nor had he expected to be instantly attracted to her.

His gaze lowered to her shapely legs as she crossed one over the other. Her skirt skimmed up her thigh, giving him a tantalizing view of a garter attached to sheer nylons. Good Lord, he marveled as she tugged on the hem to bring it back down to her knee. She was wearing a garter belt.

The muscles in his stomach tightened as his body reacted to that glimpse of lingerie. Bringing his gaze back to her face, he saw her glance at her watch. She was obviously impatient to get the interview over with, and irritation overcame his flash of desire. He told himself to keep his mind on the main reason he had made an appointment to see her.

She took the initiative away from him. "When you made the appointment with my father's secretary, I believe you said there was an urgent matter you needed to discuss. If this has to do with an article you plan to write about my father, I'm afraid you're wasting your time. The papers have already covered my father's life and his funeral quite extensively."

Nick shook his head. "I'm not here as a journalist. I came for a personal reason."

He saw something flicker in her eyes, then it was covered with a blank expression. Wherever she'd been and whatever she'd been doing since leaving Monterey, she had learned to hide her feelings.

When she didn't make any comment, he forged ahead. "I'm representing a group of men and women who support a variety of amateur athletic programs on the Monterey Peninsula. We're a nonprofit organization, not affiliated with any professional or business association. We take on a variety of projects to assist local athletes with buying equipment, uniforms, whatever need arises. A couple of months before your father died, we approached him about the use of one of the buildings Hart Corporation owns. He said he would look into the matter, but he never got back to us. You might think we're rushing things since your father passed away only three weeks ago, but there are a lot of special kids depending on us."

"Which building were you interested in?" Dionne asked.

"How familiar are you with the property belonging to the Hart Corporation?"

"More than I'd like," she said dryly, "and less than I should. Why don't you make your pitch, Mr. Lyon? Then we'll both know what you're talking about."

Before he could begin his explanation, her phone rang. With a soft sigh of exasperation, she murmured, "Excuse me."

Nick studied her as she rose and walked behind her desk, appreciating the soft, fluid lines of her body. What was it about her that captivated him? he wondered, as she picked up the phone. The severe style of her hair accentuated her high cheekbones and exposed her slender neck. The colors of her suit and shirt flattered her golden skin. The lithe grace of her movements as she leaned one slender hip against the desk made his palms itch. He listened to her voice as she spoke into the phone, not paying attention to what she was saying, only absorbing the sultry tone.

It was no use continually comparing this woman with the young girl he had known years ago. He had felt sorry for the shy teenager. This woman made his mouth water.

He saw her frown as though she wasn't pleased with what the person on the other end of the phone was saying. Bending over slightly, she jotted something down on the pad of paper on her desk. Again he noted she was left-handed, one of the many facts he hadn't known about her.

Suddenly she threw the pen down onto the desk blotter and turned her back to Nick.

Her anger was the first sign of emotion he had seen in her, other than faint amusement and cool formality. He wondered what had caused it.

As she ended the phone conversation, he heard an oddly defeated note in her voice. Turning around, she looked startled when her gaze met his, as though she had forgotten he was there. As she stared at him she straightened her spine and raised her chin, making him think she was preparing herself for another battle. Instead of returning to the sofa, she walked around to the front of the desk and perched on it, gripping the edge and crossing one ankle over the other.

"I'm sorry for the interruption." Her voice was tighter than before, although she was smiling faintly. "Where were we?"

"We were discussing the use of one of the buildings the Hart Corporation owns."

"Could you be more specific? Which building are you referring to?"

Briefly he went over the proposal they had made to her father. "As I said before, we are looking for a training facility for a bunch of kids to use. During the summer they were able to use various gyms and tracks at the high schools in Carmel, Monterey, and Pacific Grove. Now that school has started, there isn't a time for the volunteers and kids to meet that doesn't conflict with the schools' activities. Besides, it's difficult continually moving from one place to another. Three years ago your father purchased an abandoned school building from the city. It has a gymnasium that isn't being used. We approached your father about letting the athletes train there. Considering we weren't offering any financial compensation, we weren't too surprised when he told us he would think about it. We never heard from him. Apparently he wasn't interested."

"I see," she murmured. "When you didn't hear from him, you tried other facilities and have come up with zero. And that's why you've returned to the Hart Corporation, hoping that his daughter would be a softer touch than Farrell was."

Nick didn't take offense. His smile acknowledged her direct hit. "Something like that."

"I can't give you an answer until I look into the matter." Seeing his expression change, she added, "I know. That's probably what my father told you. In my case it's true. There are a number of things that have to be considered before I could agree to let your group have the gymnasium. I'm sorry if that sounds like a cop-out, but it's the best I can do. My father's holdings are vast and because of his death, they've been complicated. I've only be-gun to make a dent in the paperwork."

"Would it make any difference if I mention that the athletes are young people training for the Special Olympics?"

Dionne gave him an offended glare. "My answer has to remain the same. I won't make promises I might not be able to keep. The building might have been designated for sale or for use by someone else. I still have to look into its status no matter who you're representing."

Nick started to speak, but was interrupted again. This time it was in the solid form of the secretary with some papers needing Dionne's signature. Dionne scanned them, then signed them and handed them back. The secretary had just left when the phone rang once more. "Excuse me," Dionne murmured.

Nick watched her as she sat behind her desk and picked up the phone. Her voice was firm as she refused to consider whatever the other party was offering, but he saw her fingers fiddling with her glasses, folding and unfolding the earpieces.

The delays were sparking his irritation again. As long as they stayed in her office, they would be continually interrupted. The instant she set down the phone, he made a suggestion.

"Perhaps we could continue this discussion over lunch."

Before he even finished, she was shaking her head. "I'm afraid that's impossible, Mr. Lyon. I have a lot of work to do, which means I won't be having lunch."

"How about dinner then?"

She shook her head again. "Sorry."

This time she hadn't bothered to give an excuse. It wasn't the first time he had been turned down by a woman, but it was the first time he wanted to know why. "I'd like to have a chance to tell you more about these kids. We could also talk about old times and catch up on all the years in between."

"I understand the importance of the Special Olympics, Mr. Lyon," she said, ignoring his reference to their briefly shared past. "I will look into this property as soon as I can."

The phone rang. She put her hand on the receiver, but didn't pick it up. "If you'll leave your number with the receptionist, I'll get back to you when I've looked into the status of the school building. By Friday at the latest."

He was being dismissed, Nick thought incredulously. He pushed his long body up off the couch and stalked over to the desk, looking down at her. The phone continued to ring, but she still didn't answer it. Instead, she met his intent gaze, a puzzled expression in her eyes. His fingers curled into his palms as he resisted the urge to touch her. It was ridiculous to want to feel her smooth flesh under his hands so soon. So intensely.

Her lashes flickered, and he saw her expression change. Although she tried to hide it, the longing he remembered from years ago filled her eyes. Then it was gone. He wanted to see it again.

"Take care of your phone call," he said quietly. "I'm not leaving just yet."

Her lips tightened, but she picked up the receiver and spoke into it. Less than a minute later she replaced it. Leaning back in her chair, she gazed up at him, her fingertips and thumbs pressed together to form a triangle.

"How's your mother?" she asked quietly.

Usually quick on his feet, Nick felt as though she had knocked the floor out from under him. "She's recovering from hip surgery at the moment."

"I'm sorry to hear that."

The genuine concern in her voice surprised and warmed him. "So is she. Especially when it was her own fault. She fell over one of her sister's cats during a visit. She'll stay with my aunt in Van Nuys until she feels like making the trip back to Monterey."

"It must be difficult for her to be inactive. One of the things I remember most about her is she rarely sat for long."

Nick realized that the tension between them had vanished. "At least she has her next book to work on to keep her occupied." Smiling at the startled look in Dionne's eyes, he explained, "She's written two cookbooks and is on her third."

Dionne smiled. "Good for her. She once told me she wanted to write a cookbook but hadn't been able to find the time."

Nick knew he was gaping, but couldn't stop. It

was more than he had known about his mother until a few years ago, when she had approached him with the finished manuscript, asking his advice on how to get it published.

"Is that what you talked about when you came to the house to see her?"

Dropping her hands, she sat forward and leaned her arms on the desk. "Your mother was very kind to me. I've often thought about her."

She hadn't answered his question, and he knew she wasn't going to. He tried another one. "How about me?"

The defenses were back in place. "What about you?"

"Have you thought about me?"

A corner of her mouth lifted. "You were never kind to me," she said bluntly. "For fear of being rude I must ask you to leave, Mr. Lyon. I have an incredible amount of work to do. I will look into the matter of the school building and get back to you by Friday."

He was about to press harder, but the damn phone jangled again. Frustrated by the interruptions and her cool attitude, Nick took the only choice left to him and strode from the office.

He didn't notice the stony glare from the secretary or the resigned glance from the receptionist as he passed through the outer offices. He was too busy going over the meeting with Dionne, every word, every gesture, every expression he had seen in her eyes. Instead of curing his curiosity, the last half hour had only created more questions. Frustrated, he recalled the few facts he did know about Dionne.

Farrell Hart and his reputation were well-known. Hart had made sure of that. There wasn't a charity affair or civic function Hart hadn't taken advantage of to get publicity. He preferred the public eye to privacy, and had thrust himself into it at every opportunity. Nick had met him on a number of occasions, and had come away each time disliking the man more. Hart's fortune had been amassed in real estate, and with his ruthless wheeling and dealing, he had acquired more than just property. It was common knowledge Hart had many more enemies than friends.

As for Dionne's mother, there had been several rumors about her. The facts were that Hart had given his English wife her walking papers all the way back to England after a hefty chunk of money had been settled on her. The only stipulation had been that their daughter would remain with Hart. He had never remarried, although his affairs, some long-term, others brief, were forever in the gossip columns. He had made no attempt to be discreet.

Nick wondered what effect living with Farrell Hart had had on Dionne. Hart could be called a number of things, but paternal wasn't one of them.

As Nick unlocked the door of his car he paused for a minute, looking up at the windows of the top floor of the Hart Corporation Building. He could only imagine what life had been like for the quiet, sensitive girl left with a man like Farrell

Hart. It would be comparable to putting a delicate kitten in a cage with a vicious tiger.

Instead of going back to his small ranch in Carmel, Nick drove to the newspaper office where he used to work. For an hour he perused microfilm records of past issues. He found plenty of pictures of Farrell Hart—Hart at the Pebble Beach Golf Course, handing over checks for this or that charity, cutting a ribbon at a mall opening, shaking a politician's hand. He came across a few photos of a young blond girl with Farrell Hart. One he found particularly ridiculous. Dionne's father was holding her hand, walking her to the entrance of an elementary school building. The headline read: "MAYORAL CANDIDATE ESCORTS DAUGHTER TO FIRST DAY OF SCHOOL." Another showed an eight-year-old Dionne christening her father's new yacht. In every photo Dionne was stone faced and unsmiling, no matter what the occasion.

The only recent photo he found of her was from three weeks ago at her father's funeral. Her hand shielded part of her face, as though she'd been aware of the camera aimed at her.

Unsatisfied with what he'd found, Nick tried another source. He tapped his knuckles several times on a door with Editor In Chief printed in plain black letters on the frosted glass. A deep, gruff voice told him to go away. Nick ignored the blunt order and entered the office. Seated behind his desk, his feet propped up on the littered surface, Barry Kregor scowled at Nick.

"It's a shame a young man like you has lost his hearing," the editor said as he stabbed a pair of chopsticks into a cardboard carton. "I told you to go away."

Nick lifted a pile of papers from a chair and dropped them on the floor, then sat down. "You always say that no matter who's at the door."

"It's because I always mean it." Gesturing with the chopsticks, Barry growled, "Maybe I should electrify the doorknob. Then people would take me seriously. Just once I would like to eat my lunch in peace."

Grinning, Nick ignored the older man's bark. "Go ahead and finish your lunch. I'll wait."

The chopsticks stopped midway to the editor's mouth. "Did I hear you right? Nick Lyon will wait? You won't wait for St. Peter to open the Pearly Gates after you draw your last breath." He dropped his feet to the floor and set the carton on his desk. "What's so important you're willing to cool your heels in my office?"

"I want you to tell me what you know about Farrell Hart."

"Why?"

"You've known him a long time. You can tell me things that aren't in the files."

Barry's bushy eyebrows nearly met as he frowned. "I've known practically everybody a long time. It comes with the territory when you get old." Settling back in his chair, he added, "Farrell Hart is not the topic of conversation to have when I'm trying to eat. What do you want to know about him?"

"I'll narrow it down for you. I've just been to see his daughter." Nick briefly explained the request he had made concerning the gymnasium. "Tell me what you know about her and Hart."

One of the bushy brows raised quizzically. "If you've met her, you're already way ahead of me. I saw her at the funeral, but I didn't speak to her. As far as I know, she didn't speak to anyone. I heard she's staying at Farrell's estate. The day after the funeral she let all the staff go except for the housekeeper. Rumor is she's going to sell the place. According to the society editor, Miss Hart's turned down every social invitation sent to the house since she arrived, including one to have lunch with the society editor herself. Need I say Grace Dewitt did not take this rejection well? I sent Michaels out to the house and to the Hart Corporation to interview her, but no dice. He never even saw her. Apparently she has a couple of female dragons guarding her, one at the office and one at the estate."

"What about her life before she came back three weeks ago? She left when she was sixteen. Has she ever come back? Where has she been for fourteen years? What was she doing? Where did she go?"

Barry held up his hand. "Whoa! Those are all great questions, Nick. Basically the same ones my trusty reporter was going to ask. Why didn't you ask her when you were with her? Before you started your column, you paid your dues as a reporter. You were one of the best I've ever had working for me. You can't have forgotten how to get information from people who don't necessarily want to give it."

Nick's smile was slightly crooked. "Which is one of the reasons I started the column. I can write about what I want and not what pushy editors tell me I have to write about."

"Well, isn't that a fine thing to say to an editor," the older man said indignantly. Then he laughed. "I'll be damned. Nick, you've been bitten by the nastiest bug known to man."

"What are you talking about?"

"Dionne Hart. You're interested in her, aren't you? Oh, I don't mean as a story. I mean as a woman. From what I've heard, that man and woman thing is still going on." Without waiting for confirmation he continued, "You've never taken the easy way in anything you've set out to do, so I shouldn't be surprised you want to go after Dionne Hart."

Slapping his hands on the arms of the chair as he pushed himself up, Nick snapped, "Go back to your Mongolian pork, Barry. You're hallucinating from hunger." At the door he turned and added quietly, "Keep your reporters away from her, Barry. If the lady doesn't want to have her name in the paper, she should have that right."

"That's a lousy attitude for a journalist to have." Barry picked up the carton and waved Nick away with the chopsticks. "All right. If there's a story there, Nick, I'll leave it up to you to find it."

Nick didn't bother to contradict Barry. There wasn't going to be any story about Dionne Hart, at least none that he would write. Nick knew Barry wouldn't believe that. However, if the editor thought Nick was on to a story about Dionne, he wouldn't assign anyone else to cover her.

The sun was beginning to weaken in the sky, as Nick drove toward the Hart estate several hours later. He wondered what in blue blazes he was doing. Dionne wasn't going to be pleased to see him. Especially when he didn't have a good excuse for appearing on her doorstep.

One obstacle he thought he would have to contend with was the main gates to the estate, which had always been closed unless Hart was entertaining. Dionne apparently didn't have the same paranoia as her father, since the tall wrought iron gates stood wide open. Nick drove up the long, winding drive, then parked in front of the imposing mansion. Farrell Hart's house would have made Tara look like a beach cottage. Nick had no idea how many rooms were inside. Certainly more than one man could possibly use. The grounds were immaculately manicured, the exterior of the house pristine.

He rang the doorbell several times before the carved oak door was opened by an older woman in a black dress. Nick didn't offer his card, only his name and that he wanted to speak to Miss Hart.

The woman eyed him with suspicion as she asked him why he wanted to see Miss Hart.

"I'm an old friend," he said, stretching the truth fairly thin.

The housekeeper's expression changed dramatically, a smile erasing her wary frown. "Are you Blanche Lyon's son?"

He didn't know what that had to do with anything, but if it helped get him past Dionne's protective housekeeper, he'd use it. "Yes."

"Well, why didn't you say so?" the housekeeper said with a hint of reproof. "Dionne will certainly be willing to speak to Blanche's son."

As Nick followed the housekeeper inside, he made a mental note to have a chat with his mother real soon.

He was shown into the large living room, then the housekeeper left to find Miss Hart. While he waited, he looked around the room. The last time he had been inside the mansion had been about two years ago when he'd been invited to one of Hart's charity functions. It wasn't anything like he remembered. For one thing there wasn't as much furniture as there had been. He could see the indentions on the plush carpet where heavier pieces had once sat. Raising his gaze to the walls, he spotted areas of wallpaper that were darker than the rest, places where paintings had once hung. The priceless antiques and delicate crystal lamps that had been scattered over the tables and had made him nervous, fearing he'd knock one over, were no longer a threat. They were all gone.

Puzzled, Nick walked over to the French doors to look out over the grounds. He didn't like the thought that had immediately struck him. Dionne was selling off her father's property. It was the only answer that made any sense. And it hadn't taken her very long to start selling off Hart's expensive acquisitions. For the money. Evidently her sizable inheritance wasn't enough.

As he pulled back the curtain he saw the housekeeper cross the lawn and stop near a large fountain. She was speaking to someone hidden behind the concrete mermaid in the center of the fountain. The person, dressed in coveralls, appeared from behind the statue. Even from a distance Nick could see it wasn't a handyman or a gardener. It wasn't even a man.

It was Dionne.

Two

Gone was the sleek, aloof woman dressed in a suit and silk. Dirt was smeared across one cheek, and her blond hair was covered by a too-big, baggy golfing cap. The blue denim coveralls effectively concealed Dionne's feminine shape, but it didn't matter. Nick felt the strong, relentless pull of attraction as he stared at her. The woman in the maroon-and-gray office had intrigued him. This woman captivated him. A princess dressed in rags.

The housekeeper was speaking to Dionne and gesturing toward the house. Dionne lowered her head as though a heavy weight had just been dropped on her shoulders. Then she straightened, lifting her chin in the same defensive way he had observed in her office. Taking an orange rag out of her back pocket, she wiped her hands as she walked toward the French doors.

Nick couldn't take his gaze off her. Even in the oversized, masculine work clothes she was oddly elegant, seeming to glide over the grass. He released the curtain and stepped back as she pushed open the double doors and entered the room.

She left the doors open, either because she wanted the fresh air or an escape route. Tucking the rag back into her pocket, she faced him without any embarrassment.

"I have to give you points for persistence, Mr. Lyon. I'm sorry to disappoint you, but I haven't had time to look into the gymnasium situation yet."

She brought one hand up to the front zipper of the coveralls, and he saw a knuckle had been scraped raw. The sight of her injured skin unreasonably angered him.

"What were you doing out there?" he asked.

Exasperation tightened her mouth. "I was trying to fix the fountain."

He watched in fascination as she began to unzip the coveralls. "Why?"

"Because it doesn't work."

"I mean, why are you the one fixing it?"

She shrugged, continuing to lower the zipper. "Bernie's already doing the work of the cook and two cleaning women. She has enough to do. That leaves me."

The zipper was down to her waist, the front of the coveralls gaping open to reveal a light-colored top. "Who's Bernie?" he asked abstractedly.

As though humoring someone who wasn't too

bright, she explained patiently, "Bernice Corday My father's housekeeper. She let you in."

With an economy of movement Dionne shed the coveralls by sliding her arms out of the sleeves and shoving them down over her hips. After stepping out of them she draped the coveralls over one arm. She stood in front of him wearing a cream tank top and light blue shorts. It was an unusually cool day for September, but she had apparently chosen to dress lightly under the coveralls.

Nick's mouth went dry as he noted exactly how her breasts shaped the front of her top. He didn't think she was tryng to be provocative when she'd stripped off the coveralls. She had removed them as casually as she would a sweater or a coat. It wasn't her fault he put other connotations on her actions.

His loins tightened as she yanked off the ridiculous cap and threw it onto the couch, releasing a mass of soft corn silk curls. Then she faced him squarely, her eyes the color of the deep Pacific Ocean, cool and stormy.

Dionne couldn't control her accelerated heartbeat when she saw a fire kindle in Nick's eyes, and she silently cursed herself and him. Earlier she had been forewarned, having two days to prepare herself for his appointment. His sudden appearance at her house had caught her at a disadvantage, and there wasn't anything she could do about it.

"What do you want, Mr. Lyon?" she asked, her voice rougher than she'd intended.

"I want you to stop calling me Mr. Lyon for starters. We're not exactly strangers, Dionne."

"We're not friends either," she said forcefully. "We never have been." She had to keep the conversation on a business level. It was safer. "I'll give your request about the gymnasium the same consideration whether we're old acquaintances or strangers." She took a deep breath. "I have a lot of things left to do today. I'd appreciate your getting to the point."

"I wanted to see you."

She managed to hold his gaze, hoping her inner turmoil didn't show. After she left Monterey, she had spent a lot of time trying to forget Nicholas Lyon. At one time she'd thought the sun rose and set around him, and he hadn't even known she existed except as Farrell Hart's daughter. He had been her first painful crush, which had been fed by occasional glimpses of him at school, then eventually had died from lack of attention and, finally, his rejection. It was ironic that despite all the time she'd spent pushing him out of her mind, the moment she had seen him again, those years between might have never existed. Her pulse raced, and she was fifteen again, facing him with her heart in her throat.

Clenching her jaw, she grasped her pride tightly. She wasn't fifteen. She was twenty-nine. The years in between had taught her many things, the most important being that she was capable of making her own choices and standing by them.

Clutching the coveralls to her waist, she studied Nick, noting how maturity had added strength to his handsome features. "You really haven't changed, Nick," she said, contradicting her own thoughts. "You still charge ahead regardless of whatever might be in your path. You wanted to see me, so here you are, whether I want to see you or not. This isn't the football field at Monterey High School, and you are no longer a quarterback calling the plays."

"You've changed." He reached out and plucked the coveralls from her arms. His gaze flicked over her legs, her hips, her breasts, finally resting on her face. "And not just physically. Where did you leave the other Dionne, the shy little girl who meekly did as she was told by Daddy?"

"She grew up," she said flatly.

"Where?"

Feeling oddly exposed without the coveralls to hold, Dionne refused to let her nervousness show. "Where what?"

"Where did you do this growing up?"

She shook her head and made a scolding noise. "For someone who said he wasn't here as a journalist, you sound remarkably like a reporter doing an interview. My father enjoyed publicity. I don't. The last thing I want is to see my name in print."

He tossed the coveralls onto the couch, then grasped her upper arms. "I'm not asking about you or your past so I can write about it. You've learned how to hide your feelings, but you haven't learned much about men." His fingers tightened, bringing her closer to him. "Can't you tell when a man is attracted to you?"

She felt his heat searing her through her clothing, even though their bodies weren't touching. Her hands were spread out against his chest to hold him away from her, a feeble defense. Physically she wasn't able to keep him away. That left her with words as her only strength.

"You aren't attracted to me, Nick. You're curious about Dionne Hart, the girl who left under mysterious circumstances. You can't understand why she would leave a life of luxury behind. Your inquiring journalistic mind can't stand not knowing where she's been and what she's been doing. It's a puzzle, and you're intrigued by puzzles until they're solved. My life is not a game of twenty questions. Either my past or my present."

Relaxing his grip but not releasing her, he murmured, "You're partly right. I am curious about why you left and where you've been." He raised one hand to her face. "But you're wrong about my only being interested in Dionne Hart, the daughter of Farrell Hart. It's you, not your name or what that name represents."

Her gaze didn't falter under the intensity or the intimacy of his touch. "You'll have to live with your disappointment. There are other more fascinating things for you to study than me. You write about all sorts of different topics in your column. Surely you can find something to occupy your inquisitive nature."

"It's not my inquisitive nature that makes me

want to get to know you." His thumb brushed over the streak of dirt on her cheek, then caressed her full bottom lip. He watched her eyes widen in reaction. "You feel this, too, Dionne. I don't know about you, but I've never experienced anything like this. I don't go around wanting to tear a woman's clothes off the moment I see her."

It wasn't easy to keep from moving closer or farther away from him. Hoping she sounded more calm than she felt, she said, "I didn't come back to become involved with you or anyone else, Nick. I have too much to do in a short time. I don't need any complications."

"That's too bad, because you've already got one."

With a sudden wrenching movement she tore herself away from him. After jerking the coveralls off the couch, she headed for the open French doors. Stopping in the doorway, she looked back at him. "You turned me down once. Now I'm turning you down. We're even." She paused, then added, "Good-bye, Nick."

Nick watched her go, not following after her. She had made her feelings clear, but so had he. They were even. That was the way he wanted it between them. Equal ground.

Dionne half-expected Nick to come after her. She was relieved when he didn't—and oddly disappointed. Irritated with herself, she kept striding away from the house. When she reached the fountain, she stepped into the coveralls and zipped them up, more for warmth than because she was going to continue trying to repair the fountain.

Instead of reaching for the wrench she had been using earlier, she sat down on the wide outer rim of the fountain. She hadn't the faintest idea what she was doing tinkering with the innards of the darn fountain anyway. There wasn't a chance in a thousand she would be able to fix it. She knew as much about plumbing as she did about running a corporation. Or as much as she knew about what she was going to go with Nick Lyon.

She'd known when she came back that there was a chance she would run into him. Telling herself she wouldn't be affected one way or the other if she did see him hadn't made any difference when he'd walked into her office.

Over the years she had followed his career from writing the usual local news to the national column he had started four years ago. She had bought the book he had published a year ago as soon as it appeared in the bookstores. She had read every word and had studied the black-and-white photo of him on the book jacket.

Through his writing she had discovered a different Nick Lyon from the boy she had known in high school. His sense of humor surprised her, especially when he used it to make a point in his column. His writing had a subtle, dry wit that kept the reader's attention while he wrote about everything from breakfast cereal to the plight of the homeless.

She admired his dedication to fighting unpopular causes through the written word. It was another side of him, a sensitive side that cared about injustices and inequality. Many people wished things were different but didn't do anything about them. Nick tried to change them, or at least make people aware of the alternatives.

Dionne brushed away an insect buzzing around her head and wondered what she was going to do if Nick meant what he had said about getting to know her. Ever since she had returned to Monterey, she had been involved in trying to settle her father's estate. She still had a long way to go before all the debts were paid and she could return to San Francisco. The way things were going, she was going to have to ask for more than a short leave of absence from the school where she taught special education.

When her father's lawyer had phoned to tell her about her father's fatal heart attack, she had planned to stay in Monterey only long enough to attend the funeral. She hadn't expected him to leave her anything, figuring he had written her off as easily as he had her mother. When she learned she had inherited his entire estate, she planned to sign it over to a charity. She hadn't taken anything from her father since she left his house fourteen years ago. She certainly didn't want his money or his property now.

It wasn't that easy. Instead of vast wealth, her father's estate held only formidable debts. The simplest way to meet the liabilities was to sell the properties held by the Hart Corporation. But businesses could fail and people would be out of work if she merely sold buildings out from under the people who were occupying them, without giving these people a chance to try to purchase them.

She turned her head to look at the French doors. Nick had closed them. She hoped he had left too. Just when she thought she had all the problems she could possibly handle, Nick Lyon presented her with another. His reasons might not be clear, but the fact remained that he appeared to be interested in her. Still she wasn't convinced he wanted to see her for personal and not professional reasons. He hadn't had any trouble resisting her fourteen years ago. She remembered the reporters who used to hang around her father like persistent bloodhounds sniffing out a juicy story. Most of the time Farrell Hart had been more than happy to supply them with facts or fiction, either about himself or his latest business deal. Her father had lapped up the attention like a thirsty Doberman.

Publicity was the last thing she wanted. Somehow she had to keep Nick and all the other reporters from writing about her. She had managed to keep a low profile so far.

Dionne sighed wearily. There was also the situation with her father's mistress. Until she could get a final accounting of her indebtedness, confronting Leah Buckner and her demands only led to distasteful scenes Dionne could do without. She couldn't give the woman any money, even if she felt her father's latest mistress deserved it. Leah Buckner claimed her two-year-old son was Farrell Hart's, which certainly complicated matters.

Since she wasn't accomplishing anything by just sitting there, Dionne picked up her tools. She walked back to the house, this time to the back door. As she put the toolbox in a hall cupboard, she could hear sounds of activity in the kitchen. Heaven help her, she thought. Bernie was baking again. The housekeeper had been using her culinary skills to occupy her mind and hands while deciding what to do now that Dionne had given her her notice. The problem with Bernie's choice of therapy was she expected Dionne to eat the results.

Bernice Corday had been one of the few members of Farrell Hart's household staff who had managed to put up with his demanding ways all these years. Letting Bernie go was the hardest thing Dionne had had to do, but it had been necessary. There simply wasn't enough money to keep the house going, which meant Bernie would have to find another position. The housekeeper refused to leave immediately as the rest of the staff had, insisting on staying as long as Dionne was there.

Standing in the doorway, Dionne let her gaze roam around the kitchen. Out of all the rooms in the mansion, including her own bedroom, this was the only one she was vaguely comfortable in. To her surprise, her bedroom had been left as it had been when she lived there. Even her clothes were in the closets. The only concession to time was the plastic covers over them. The rest of the house had been almost the same, too, a showcase of antiques and expensive furniture purchased by an overrated decorator her father had hired when he first bought the house.

Even though she had been there three weeks, Dionne still felt strange being back in the house. She had never expected to return. Certainly not this way.

Feeling a need to work off some tension, Nick stopped at the racquet club in Carmel to put in a couple of hours of strenuous exercise. All he accomplished was losing two games. In the locker room later he wasn't surprised to see several members of the Special Olympics support group he was involved in. Like him, the men were avid racquetball and tennis players. Nick answered their questions about his meeting with Dionne Hart, admitting that he hadn't gotten a firm commitment, but adding that she hadn't said no either. One of the men joked about Farrell Hart's daughter not being a good sport. She must be just like her old man, another said. If there wasn't any money to be made, Miss Hart wouldn't be interested. That remark led to others, and Nick left before he did something stupid, like punch out every man who opened his mouth.

He was unaware that one of the men who had been listening to the banter was a reporter.

He learned that bit of information the next morning. As he read the morning paper with his first cup of coffee, he almost choked when he saw

Dionne's name in the local sportswriter's weekly column. Evidently Barry hadn't instructed the sports reporters that Dionne Hart was off-limits. This one gave a colorful account of the conversation in the locker room, bending the facts occasionally to embellish the story. The discussion had been blown out of proportion and slanted poorly in Dionne's direction. The fact that the athletes concerned were participants in the Special Olympics was played up, adding weight to the columnist's references to Miss Hart's lack of charity and compassion.

Listed as a participant in the conversation was Nick Lyon, writer of "The Lyon's Roar."

Tossing the paper aside in disgust, Nick looked up the number for Farrell Hart's home. The housekeeper answered, telling Nick that Dionne had left early for the office. Since it was only seven o'clock, he had to wait an hour before the switchboard of the Hart Corporation answered. When he did get through to the overly charming receptionist, he was told Miss Hart was not available. That could mean either Dionne actually wasn't there, or she didn't want to talk to him.

Furious, Nick grabbed his car keys, intent on having a little heart-to-heart chat with Barry Kregor. The editor hadn't come right out and promised not to print anything about Dionne, but he had said if there was a story, he would leave it to Nick to write it.

When he arrived at the Monterey Herald Building, Nick wasn't able to see Barry. The editor-in-chief wasn't in his office. Since he couldn't vent his anger on the editor, Nick went in search of the sportswriter. Before he could locate him, he overheard a reporter yell for a photographer to get a move on. There were picketers marching in front of the Hart Corporation Building.

Nick wasn't far behind the reporter and the photographer. When he parked behind their van, he recognized other reporters from regional papers milling around and snapping pictures of about ten people, carrying placards and strolling in a sloppy circle around the entrance of the building. There was even a reporter from Salinas.

The signs had various slogans, such as, Hart Corporation Has No Heart and Dionne Hart is a Bad Sport.

Nick guessed the local fanatics had been busy since the morning paper had hit their doorsteps, managing to gather enough disgruntled supporters on short notice. Nick's problem was going to be convincing Dionne he hadn't been responsible for either the article or the protesters.

Getting out of his car, he slammed the door and leaned against it. Having Dionne see his name in an article about her was bad enough. Even if she didn't normally read the sports section, someone was bound to mention the column or the ruckus in front of the building. The pickets weren't going to endear him to her if she thought he had been partly to blame.

As he started toward the building he saw the crush of reporters dart to one side like a school of fish. He cursed under his breath when he caught a glimpse of Dionne's blond hair in the midst of the crowd. Quickening his stride, he hurried toward the throng of protesters and reporters. As he pushed people aside he saw Dionne throw her hand up to shield her face as cameras and microphones were pointed at her.

She managed to get into the building with the help of several security guards who rushed to her assistance. Following close behind, Nick caught a glimpse of her as she pushed open a door off the lobby and disappeared inside.

The security guards returned to the front entrance, apparently more concerned about the crowds of people outside than anyone inside. Nick crossed the lobby and saw Dionne had gone into the ladies' rest room. He pushed open the door anyway. Nothing short of a barbed wire fence would have kept him out.

Dionne was standing in front of a row of sinks and mirrors, her head bowed as she gripped the sides of a basin so tightly, her knuckles were white. She was wearing a dark blue coatdress with several strands of gold and pearl necklaces draped around her neck, falling almost to the black belt around her slender waist.

When he quietly said her name, she whirled around. His heart ached when he saw tears shimmering in her eyes.

Three

As Dionne struggled to recover her composure
Nick fought the urge to pull her into his arms and
comfort her. Since he was probably the last person she would allow to touch her, he settled for
standing a couple of feet away from her. Words of
apology were on the tip of his tongue, but he
didn't say them. He doubted she would want to
hear them right then.

"Unless," she said, her voice tight with sup-
pressed anger, "you have an uncontrollable urge
to powder your nose, I suggest you leave, Nick.
Some of the women employees might not appreciate finding a man in here."

"You have a right to be angry, Dionne, but not
at me. I didn't have anything to do with the article or that scene outside."

She said nothing, but he could see she didn't

believe him. "Dammit, Dionne. It isn't my fault that jackass reporter wrote that garbage."

"It was only a coincidence he knew all about your visit to the Hart Corporation?"

"Some of the members of the group I told you about happened to be at the racquetball club. They wanted to know how the meeting went, and I told them you were going to look into the matter."

"Something got lost along the way—like the truth."

He couldn't disagree with that. I'll walk with you to your office. The security guards have gone back to the entrance."

She shook her head. "No. I don't need an escort. Why don't you go join your friends outside? I'm sure someone will give you a sign to carry. Who knows? Maybe you'll even get your picture in the paper."

That did it. He no longer felt like apologizing. Closing the distance between them, he gripped her arms and pulled her toward him. Her lips parted in protest, but before she could make a sound, he lowered his head and kissed her.

Desire replaced Dionne's anger. Hunger overcame her humiliation. She clenched her fingers into a fist, catching some of the material of his khaki photographer's vest as riotous feelings spun through her. When he slanted his mouth and broke open her lips to taste her more fully, she couldn't stop her sigh of pleasure. Her fingers loosened and smoothed over his hard chest to his shoulders, then around his neck, bringing her breasts against him.

The place didn't matter. Whether they were in a woman's lavatory or alone on a sun-soaked beach, she knew her reactions would be the same. The need to touch and taste, to savor and sample overcame everything else.

At last Nick raised his head. With his hands framing her face, he simply looked at her for a long moment.

Dionne dropped her arms and touched her lips with her fingertips until she realized what she was doing. With the sink behind her and Nick directly in front of her, she couldn't put any distance between them. She had to settle for wrapping her arms around her waist.

"You could have just told me to shut up," she said quietly. "You didn't have to kiss me."

"Yes, I did."

Because she wanted him to kiss her again, she abruptly turned around. Needing to occupy her hands, she ran the cold water and washed her hands. As she dried them Nick realized she wasn't going to say anything.

"Dionne, I won't apologize for kissing you, but I will say I'm sorry for the scene outside although I'm not responsible for it."

She met his gaze in the mirror. "Are you saying you weren't part of the charming scene in that locker room? That the reporter put your name in for local color? Or was your name simply a typographical error?" She crumpled the paper towel and tossed it into the waste bin, then turned to face him. "It seems a bit odd that the reporter would just make up your name as one of the guys who was having so much fun at my expense."

Her lips thinned as she remembered some of the things that had been written about her. "But they weren't just discussing me, were they? They were making jokes about me in a smelly, sweaty locker room. I don't think I deserved that."

"I never made any jokes about you, Dionne."

"So you weren't responsible for the crack about Dionne Hartless? Or perhaps you contributed the remark about how I must have a profound dislike of jockstraps."

"Even though you haven't seen me in years," he said quietly, a dangerous edge to his voice, "you should know I didn't say any of those things."

"All I know is there are reporters nipping at my heels like rabid dogs. The phone started ringing at the house almost before the ink had dried on the morning paper. I couldn't stand it so I came to the office. When I arrived here, it was almost as bad. I went out to take care of some business, and when I got back, I ran into the mess outside. Anyone would think I'd desecrated a national shrine. You sports enthusiasts are somewhat fanatical, aren't you?"

"The article was a piece of fluff written by an idiot. He thought he was being funny while trying to shame you into letting the kids use the gymnasium. Apparently a few nut cases took the column seriously and decided to stomp around outside with some signs to get attention from the media. The whole thing will blow over in a couple of days."

Her lips curved into a mockery of a smile. "Until the reporters find something else to write about. I learned early that the name Hart can stir up all sorts of storms. All I can do is ride them out, but I don't have to like them."

"Not all reporters are like that sports columnist. Most try to report fairly and accurately."

"I realize they have a job to do. I just don't want them doing it around me."

Sadness tinged her eyes, and he again struggled not to touch her. "Your father would have enjoyed the spectacle and might have even given a press conference or two."

"You're probably right," she said with a note of resigned humor in her voice. "If you're making a list of the ways I'm different from my father, add that one. The last thing I want is press coverage."

The door burst open and two women entered, laughing. When they saw Dionne, they abruptly ceased laughing, apparently aware of who she was. When they then saw Nick, they simply stared with their mouths open.

Rather than bother making any explanations or excuses, Nick clasped Dionne's hand and pulled her out of the rest room. As soon as the door whooshed closed after them, he began walking in the opposite direction from the main entrance.

"Do you know another way out of the building?" he asked.

"Yes. Why?"

"You said your office is deluged with phone calls, so let's get out of here. We need to talk."

Not wanting to confront the mass of people out front, Dionne stepped ahead of him, leading the way to a door farther down the hall. His fingers tightened when she tried to pull her hand from his hold as she led him through various passageways. When they reached the back entrance, a solitary security guard nodded respectfully to Dionne. He was about to open the door for them, when Nick tugged her to a stop.

"You stay here with the guard," he said. "I'll go get my car and bring it around back to pick you up. It looks like everyone's attention is only at the main entrance."

"I have a better idea," she said. "You go to your car, and I'll go to mine."

His eyes darkened with determination. "We're going to have that talk, and we can't have it here without being interrupted every five minutes."

Aware of the security guard, Dionne said emphatically, "I can't think of anything left to talk about, Nick. All I want to do is to get to my father's house without any of those reporters yelling questions at me or taking pictures."

"What makes you think they won't be waiting for you at the estate?"

It was obvious by her stricken expression, she hadn't thought of that. With a defeated sigh she leaned against the wall.

The guard looked from one to the other with a puzzled expression. When Nick took Dionne's arm, the guard put his hand on the door latch, hesitating to open the door until he was sure they were actually going out this time. They did, and he touched the bill of his cap as they passed him.

Once outside, Nick asked, "Where's your car?"

"It's in the parking lot beside the building, but one of the reporters saw me get out of it. Someone is bound to be watching it."

Nick guided her away from the building in the opposite direction from where his own car was parked. Since he was walking quickly and hadn't released her arm, Dionne practically had to run to keep up with him.

"Where are we going?"

"We're going to the Row."

"The Row?" she asked. "You mean Cannery Row?"

"We can duck into one of the restaurants and stay out of the way until the reporters and the picketers get tired and leave."

Since she couldn't come up with any other alternative for eluding the reporters, Dionne didn't see that she had a choice but to go along with him. There was one small complaint she was going to have to make, though.

Stopping abruptly, she planted her hands on her hips. Nick jerked to a halt. "What's the matter?"

"If you expect me to go anywhere with you, you're going to have to slow down. I'm not one of your jock friends who likes to jog wherever they go."

Chuckling, he placed her arm through the crook of his and shortened his steps to match hers. "Is this better?"

Better wasn't the word she would have chosen. Her arm was pressed against his side, and her hip occasionally grazed his. "It depends on how far we have to walk."

He glanced down at her. "Don't you know where Cannery Row is?"

"Of course I do," she said indignantly. "It's on Monterey Bay." Waving her hand in several directions, she murmured, "It's somewhere over there."

He took her hand and moved it to indicate the correct location. "That's where the Bay is. The Row is one block from here. Another half a block to get to the restaurant I have in mind." Releasing her hand, he continued walking. "I can't believe you don't know where the Bay is located. Even if you haven't been back in the area for a long time, you should have remembered Fisherman's Wharf and Cannery Row. They haven't moved."

Looking straight ahead, she couldn't help the trace of defensiveness in her voice. "I've never been to Cannery Row or Fisherman's Wharf, but I know they're located on the Bay."

Nick stared at her, shocked that Dionne had never been to the Row or the Wharf. He couldn't count all the times he had gone to the wharf area as a child, a teenager, and as an adult. The area was his favorite aside from his ranch. His reasons for going to the Row and the Wharf had changed over the years, but not his enjoyment of either place. He had been one of the first ones in line when the Monterey Bay Aquarium opened in 1984.

While they walked, Nick noticed Dionne kept

glancing around nervously, as though making sure they weren't being followed by the relentless reporters. Through her actions he was getting a small taste of what it was like to feel the pressure of continual public scrutiny.

The restaurant he took her to was one of the smaller, lesser-known establishments. It wasn't part of Cannery Row, but was on one of the side streets leading inland. The sign over the front entrance stated Canaveri's, as did the bright orange neon sign in the long front window, which was partly covered by a profusion of healthy hanging plants.

Nick held the door open for Dionne and followed her in. A short, plump woman in a white peasant blouse and red full skirt hurried from behind the counter, smiling broadly when she saw Nick.

"Nicky! It's about time you come to see Momma." After giving Nick a big hug and a noisy kiss on his cheek, the woman glanced at Dionne. "And you brought a friend. How nice."

"Momma, this is Dionne."

Nick saw the shock on Dionne's face when Momma gave her a hug as well. "Welcome, welcome, Dionne."

"Thank you. You have a charming restaurant, Mrs. Canaveri."

"Call me Momma, please." The gregarious woman glanced around the restaurant, sighing heavily. "We work hard but Papa is better at the stove than the cash register." She threw her hands up in the air, as if tossing off her worries. "You did not come here to hear my troubles. What would you like? Fettucini, lasagne?"

Nick put his arm around Momma. "Dionne's never had one of your thick slices of apple pie. Do you think you can do something about that?"

Momma couldn't have been more pleased. "I just took a batch of pies out of the oven. You sit down. I'll bring the pie and some coffee."

As Dionne sat down at a square table covered in a red-and-white-checkered tablecloth, she wondered why Nick had introduced her by her first name only. She had the feeling it wasn't an oversight. For some reason Nick didn't want Momma Canaveri to know who she was.

Nick sat down across from her and leaned back in his chair. "I suppose I should warn you about the pie. Momma thinks a normal piece is practically half the pie. Don't eat it too fast or she'll automatically bring you another slab. If you manage to finish the first one, she'll try to talk you into seconds. When you turn it down, don't let her tears and her sad voice sway you or you'll never be able to walk out of here without eating the other half of the pie."

"She seems to know you very well."

"I used to come here quite often when I lived in Monterey. Now that I live on the ranch, I don't get the chance to eat here much."

Dionne couldn't hide her astonishment. "You live on a ranch?"

"In Carmel Valley." When he smiled, small lines

at the corners of his eyes deepened. "To a Texan, calling my spread a ranch would probably be blasphemy since it's only four acres of land. But to me, it's perfect. The house is Spanish-style with a tiled roof and sits at the bottom of a foothill. There's a small stream running through the property and a corral for my three horses. The best part of the location is that I can't see any of my neighbors, so it seems as though the ranch is remote."

Dionne smiled at the glow of enthusiasm and excitement in his eyes and voice. "You're full of surprises, Nick."

"In what way?"

She regretted blurting out what she'd been thinking. His lifestyle was none of her business, and he might turn around and ask her about her own. "It was just a figure of speech. Forget it."

"You started it. Now finish it. I'm interested in hearing your answer."

She fiddled with her fork, irritated with herself for saying anything in the first place. Since she had started it, she was going to have to finish it.

"Your choice of career for one thing. I wouldn't have thought you would become a journalist. It seems a bit . . . tame for you. Now you're telling me you live on a ranch. Both your occupation and your lifestyle are more solitary than I would have expected you to want."

He sat back once again, watching her with an intensity that should have had her out of her chair and running from the restaurant and him.

"It's nice to know you've been thinking about me. What kind of life did you think I had?"

She shrugged, trying for a casualness she was far from feeling. "I've never thought much about you or your lifestyle until now," she lied.

Momma bustled up to the table with gigantic portions of fragrant apple pie on dinner plates. After they were plopped down with a flourish, the cheerful woman brought them large cups of coffee.

"I told Papa you were here, Nicky. He said not to leave until he can come out. He's decorating a cake for a wedding."

Nick nodded. "We'll be here a while."

Momma smiled warmly at Dionne. "You enjoy Momma's pie now. Nicky likes women with substance, not style." Then she left them, stopping at several other tables to chat with customers.

Dionne slowly picked up her fork, staring at the formidable piece of pie in front of her. "Nick," she murmured, "I can't possibly eat all of this."

He grinned and cut into his pie. "Just do the best you can. Remember, eat slowly like you're savoring every bite."

Dionne glanced over toward the counter were Momma was polishing a glass. The older woman was looking at them, a broad smile on her face. Returning her attention to the pie, Dionne cut a piece with her fork.

Nick watched her eyes slowly close as she reveled in the burst of flavor in her mouth. Her expression when she reopened her eyes sent hot flames licking along his veins. All the years he had eaten Momma's apple pie, he had never considered it a sensual experience. Until now. He watched in fascination as Dionne's tongue slid across her bottom lip to catch a small flake of crust. His fingers tightened on his fork as his blood surged through his loins. He thought he had experienced every gambit of desire in the past, but he'd never felt this gut-wrenching need from a simple, innocent gesture.

Setting down the fork, he picked up his cup of coffee and took a sip, nearly burning his tongue. It didn't do anything to quench his thirst for her. Grasping for something to take his mind off the urge to run his tongue over her lip as she had, he returned to the subject they'd been discussing before Momma brought the pie.

"You were surprised about where I live and what I do. At least you know that much about me. All I know about you is that until you were sixteen, you lived in your father's house. Now you're back at the Hart Estate, but I don't know where you've been in the years between. No one does."

Stalling, Dionne ate another small bite of pie under the watchful eye of Momma. "Bernie told me there was a great deal of gossip going around after I left Monterey. I can't imagine why. Very few people knew me other than as Farrell Hart's daughter, so it seems strange anyone would care if I left or stayed."

Nick realized she really believed no one had been affected by her sudden disappearance all those years ago. "It's human nature to want to solve a mystery. You were only sixteen when you left and, like it or not, you are Farrell Hart's daughter. That's two good reasons why people are curious about you."

"And you're one of them," she said bluntly. "You're also the last person I would tell my life story to, considering you make your living writing for a newspaper."

He held open the two sides of his vest. "See? No tape recorder or notebooks. Whatever you tell me is just between you and me."

"Then why do you keep patting your pockets?" Startled, he blinked. "Do I?"

"I haven't counted, but it was enough to make me wonder what you were doing." She smiled faintly. "I wondered if you were secretly playing with a tape recorder's on-and-off switch."

"You watch too many spy movies," he said with amusement. "It's much simpler than that. I quit smoking six months ago and occasionally I feel the need for a cigarette. Like when I'm in a situation when a cigarette would give me something to do with my hands—other than what I would like to do and shouldn't."

Her eyes met his, startled and slightly alarmed as she correctly guessed his meaning. She wished he wouldn't look at her that way, making her feel as though he were already touching her.

Pushing his plate away, he rested his arms on the table and leaned forward. "What about you, Dionne? What vices have you discovered since leaving Monterey?"

Surprising them both, she smiled freely and naturally for the first time. "I don't know if it qualifies as a vice, but I have a disgusting weakness for caramel corn."

"Caramel corn? Sticky popcorn with nuts and stuff in it?"

She almost laughed at his description. " 'Fraid so."

"That doesn't sound like such a bad vice. Maybe different, but it's healthier than smoking."

Her mouth twisted. "Tell my hips that," she muttered, then immediately regretted the quip when his eyes gleamed.

"My pleasure."

His attention was drawn away from her when a man coming out of the kitchen hailed him from across the room. "Here comes Papa," Nick murmured under his breath.

Dionne turned her head and saw a tall, extremely thin man weaving his way through the tables, heading in their direction. He was dressed completely in white from his T-shirt and denim pants, to his apron and a sailor hat perched on his balding head. His smile was as warm and welcoming as Momma's.

Nick stood up and was again wrapped in an affectionate hug. "Nicky, it is so good to see you. Momma said you brought a pretty girl with you."

Nick made the introductions, once more omitting Dionne's last name. Before she knew what was happening, she was whisked out of her chair by Papa and hugged. Dionne found herself hug-

ging him back, though only she knew how unusual the gesture was for her to make.

When he eventually released her, Papa insisted
she sit back down and eat her pie. "Momma won't
like it if I keep you from finishing your pie." He
turned to Nick and slapped him on the shoulder.
"It's good to see you, Nicky. You don't come around
near enough anymore."

"I'll try to come more often, Papa. Listen, I have
a favor to ask. Could I borrow your van to take
Dionne home? I'll bring it back in an hour or so."

"Sure, sure. Take as long as you want," Papa
said without bothering to ask Nick why he wanted
it. He dove his hand into a pocket under the
apron and brought out a set of keys. Grinning
widely, Papa added, "Bring her back again, Nicky.
She hugs good."

As Nick accepted the keys from Papa he wished
he could say the same with some authority. Papa
had known Dionne two seconds, and she had
responded to his friendly embrace. She had known
Nick a lot longer and hadn't reacted that naturally
with him. Maybe he needed to get an apron.

Dionne waited until Papa had returned to the
kitchen before she asked Nick why he was bor-
rowing Papa's van.

"If there are any reporters staking out your
house, they won't be expecting you to come home
in a van."

"My father's house," she corrected him. "What
about my car?"

"I'll see that it's brought to your house."

"My father's house," she repeated.

"It's your house now."

Not for long, she thought grimly. Thinking about Nick's plan, she decided if going in Papa Canaveri's van would get her back to the estate without drawing reporters, then she would go with him.

He had solved one problem, but she had another. "I have one small obstacle before I can leave."

"What's that?"

She glanced down at her plate with its half-finished pie. "How do we get out of here without hurting Momma's feelings? I can't possibly finish this."

Nick looked around for the woman in question. Momma was at the door hugging a couple who were about to leave. He leaned over the table and whispered, "I guess we're going to have to resort to my sneaky retreat."

Dionne leaned forward too. "Whatever it is, I'll do it."

"Fold your napkin over once, then spread it out beside your plate. When Momma isn't looking, you flip the pie into the napkin and fold the edges over. I usually tuck it under my jacket and saunter out casually."

She looked down at her dress. "I might have to make a few changes to your sneaky retreat. Would tucking it into my purse qualify as a sneaky retreat?"

"Absolutely." He looked up. "Quick. Momma's heading for the kitchen. Now's our chance."

Feeling as if she were stealing the crown jewels,

Dionne quickly followed his instructions and slid the remainder of her slice into her napkin. She didn't want to think of what the pie would do to the interior of her purse. As she tucked the mushy bundle into it, Nick was stealthily sliding his into one of the pockets of his vest. He tossed some money onto the table, then took her arm and helped her up.

"Papa's van is out back," he said, lowering his head to whisper in her ear, "which means we have to go through the kitchen. Pretend you're invisible. One of Momma's hugs and I'm going to have a helluva mess in my pocket."

Dionne bit her lip to keep from laughing as Nick guided her through the tables. Luckily both Papa and Momma were having a colorful argument with a delivery man over a box of produce when they walked through the kitchen. Nick tiptoed around them in an exaggerated fashion, placing one finger over his lips to warn her not to say a word. Dionne had to struggle to keep from laughing as they stole through the kitchen like two thieves.

Seated in the van, she happened to meet Nick's eyes as he shut his door. She saw the amusement dancing there and started laughing.

When Dionne laughed, Nick's breath caught in his throat. Her laughter filled the cab of the van, making him think of musical chimes and soft summer breezes. It was the first time he had ever heard her laugh. He didn't want it to be the last.

The ride to the Hart estate was bumpy and

bouncy, not because the road was in poor condition, but because the springs and shocks in the van were nonexistent. Dionne thought her teeth were being shaken loose, and worried that the coiled springs in the seat were becoming a permanent part of her anatomy. It was impossible to talk, so neither even tried.

Nick had been right. There were two cars parked outside the gates of the estate. Neither of the two men leaning against one of the cars even glanced at the van as Nick drove between the brick pillars. He stopped in front of the house but didn't shut off the motor.

"Will you be all right?" he asked her.

"Sure. I'll unplug the phones, and Bernie will barricade the doors."

"Those picketers were wrong about your being a bad sport. You've been a very good sport with Momma and Papa Canaveri. They can be a little overpowering for some people."

"They were charming. As for being a good sport, you're the only one who's never thought so. The sports reporter was right about one of the things he said. I've never been interested in athletic competition." She looked at the house, her father's house. "I don't consider winning as important as some people do."

He caught the bitterness in her voice. "Maybe you've been exposed to the wrong sports." Leaning across her, he unlatched her door. "We'll correct that tomorrow night. I'll pick you up at seven-thirty. Dress casual."

"You've got to be kidding. I'm not going any-where tomorrow night. I have men with cameras and tape recorders following me, remember?"

"I'll take care of the reporters. I'm going to go have a friendly chat with the editor of the *Herald* and have him call off the dogs."

"Why should he do that for you?"

He smiled. "I can be very charming when I want to. Just trust me." He held out his hand. "Give me your car keys."

"Why?"

"So I can have your car delivered to you. I sup-pose I could try to hot-wire it, but it's one of the few things I never learned during my misspent youth."

Good Lord, she thought. She'd forgotten all about her car. She opened her purse to dig out her keys. Her fingers touched the napkin-wrapped apple pie. She took it out first and placed it in his out-stretched hand. A few second later she piled the keys on top of it, then climbed down off the front seat and shut the door.

She placed her hands on the open window frame. "About tomorrow night. I'd rather not take the chance of going out where people might see us."

"Tough. I'll be here at seven-thirty." Grinning suddenly, he added, "I'll bring the caramel corn."

Dionne had to drop her hands and step back when he put the van in gear and drove away without giving her a chance to refuse him.

Four

Dionne stared after the van as it rambled down the driveway and out of sight. Nick hadn't given her a choice about going out with him. To her amazement she didn't mind as much as she should. Ever since she had escaped her father's domination, she had rigidly refused to let anyone direct her life. So why didn't she mind Nick's cavalier attitude? she wondered.

She placed her hand on her stomach as though to hold back the sickening clutch of fear mixed with panic. The feeling was familiar, like an old enemy she had fought many times. The difference was that this time it wasn't fear of the unknown, as it had been when she'd gotten on the bus to San Francisco fourteen years ago, scared out of her mind at the giant step she was taking.

This time she knew it was her growing feelings

for Nicholas Lyon that were scaring her silly. She hadn't imagined the attraction building between them and she didn't know what to do about it. An affair with Nick would be all she could have, a brief sexual encounter that would devastate her when it ended.

She was afraid she would find herself needing Nick if she continued seeing him. She didn't want to need anyone. She had learned early she could only count on herself, rely on her own judgment. Depending on someone else for her happiness would only lead to pain.

For so many years she had been in control, making all the decisions in every aspect of her life. Now she was floundering around like a fish dropped into a strange sea.

When Nick had kissed her, she had felt like Sleeping Beauty waking up after a long sleep. Except this wasn't a fairy tale. Nick made her feel alive in a way that was frightening and exciting all at the same time.

She shook her head. She didn't need anyone. She had managed just fine on her own, and that was the way she would continue. On her own. She frowned, adding the one word that described the way she lived. Alone.

She ran up the steps as though someone were chasing her. Using the key her father's lawyer had given her, she let herself into the house. Her footsteps sounded unusually loud on the parquet floor in the empty foyer. The sumptuous Oriental rug that had once graced the entrance would have muffled the sound if it hadn't been sold.

Bernie would be in the kitchen at this time of day. Dionne would have preferred going directly to her room to change and be alone to think, but she needed to let Bernie know she was home. She headed for the kitchen and, as usual, found Bernie at the stove.

"Hi, Bernie."

The older woman dropped the peeler she'd been using on a small mound of carrots. Placing her hand on her heart, she gasped, "Good Lord, Dionne. You scared me. I didn't hear your car." She pointed to the back door. "You usually park at the rear of the house."

"I didn't drive home."

Bernie picked up the peeler, then walked over to the sink to wash it off. "How did you get home then?"

"Someone gave me a ride."

"Did you have car trouble?"

Dionne shook her head. "There were a pack of reporters and people picketing the building. I couldn't get to my car."

"Why are people picketing the Hart Corporation?"

Dionne explained about the article in the sports section of the newspaper. "Nick Lyon said he was going to talk to the editor of the paper about calling off the reporters."

Bernie nodded. "Good for him. You know, I read his column every week." She chuckled. "He can make the simplest thing like buying toothpaste hilarious."

"I must have missed that one," Dionne murmured, sorry she had brought up Nick's name. To change the subject, she said, "Is that dinner you're making? It smells delicious."

"It's just a little roast. It'll be ready at six. Why don't you sit down and relax? I'll put water on for a nice cup of tea. I hope you don't mind, but I unplugged all the phones. They just kept ringing and ringing."

Sitting down in a chair, Dionne kicked off her shoes and sighed. "You beat me to it. It was going to be the second thing I did when I got home. Taking off my shoes was number one."

"Did those people give you a hard time at your father's office?"

"They were acting as though I've outlawed sports."

"Such a fuss," Bernie muttered impatiently. "If they knew the problems you already had to deal with, perhaps they would be more understanding about why you haven't given them the school gymnasium outright just because they want it."

Dionne smiled. Bernie's loyalty was commendable, considering she had been given her notice. "The last thing I want is for the reporters to learn about the condition of Farrell's estate. Once prospective buyers know how desperate I am to sell the property, I'll end up having to practically give it away. I need every penny I can get to pay off the mountain of debts Farrell left behind."

Bernie took a covered roasting pan out of the oven and set it on the counter. "Has the realtor had any response on this house?"

"A couple of nibbles but no solid bites." Dionne hated the circumstances her father had put her in. She had to hurt innocent people because of his carelessness with his investments. "I'll try to give you as much notice as I can, Bernie."

Bernie slowly turned around. Clutching the hot pad between her hands, she looked at Dionne with a worried expression on her usually serene face. "Not all of the phone calls were from reporters today, Dionne. Do you remember me telling you about my friend in New Mexico who's been asking me to come for a visit?"

"I remember. You mentioned her when I told you I was going to have to sell the house."

Bernie plucked nervously at the hot pad. "Well, Agnes called today and asked me to come live with her. Her son has gotten married and now she lives in her big house all by herself. She said there's plenty of room."

Considering it was such a perfect solution for Bernie, Dionne wondered why she didn't sound happier about it. "Do you think you would enjoy living with her?"

Bernie nodded. "We've been friends a long time. She would be good company." She hesitated, then added, "She wanted me to come within a week, but I hate to leave you until you have everything settled here."

Dionne walked to Bernie and put her hands on

the housekeeper's shoulders. "I'm glad you have someplace to go, Bernie. You go ahead and make your plans to leave whenever it's convenient for you. I'll be fine."

Bernie looked uncertain. "Are you sure?"

Dionne nodded. "I hated telling you I was selling the house, because it meant you would have to leave. This has been your home for as long as I can remember. It can't be easy for you to go."

"It's been a difficult house at times. Your father wasn't an easy man to please."

"That's true." It was also the understatement of the year. Dionne dropped her hands. "I don't know how you put up with him all these years."

Bernie shrugged. "Under that hard crust your father presented to the world was a very lonely man. I guess I felt sorry for him. Plus this is a lovely house. I've been very comfortable here."

Unwilling to discuss her father, Dionne picked up a hot pad and lifted the cover off the roasting pan. "A little roast?" she exclaimed. "This looks big enough to feed a small army."

Bernie accepted the change in subject. "What we need is a man with a healthy appetite. You should have asked Blanche's son in for dinner."

Dionne could have told her Nick had a healthy appetite, but it wasn't strictly for food. Pushing away thoughts of Nick, she measured tea leaves into the china teapot and poured boiling water into it.

Bernie had one more phone call to report to Dionne. "That awful Buckner woman called again.

When I told her you weren't here, she said to give you a message. On the advice of her attorney, she's made an appointment with a doctor for blood tests for her son."

Dionne gazed down in the teapot as she stirred the leaves, creating a small whirlpool. She felt like the tea leaves, as though she were being pulled into a deep, swirling mass, never to rise again. "Does she want me to call her back?"

"She just said to give you the message."

Dionne poured the tea into two china cups. "I'll take this upstairs with me. I'd like to change my clothes."

The housekeeper nodded. "Why don't you take a nice warm bath to help you relax? Dinner won't be ready for a while."

Dionne shook her head. "I have a few phone calls to make and some papers to go over after dinner. If I take a bath now, I'll be too sleepy to get any work done."

Her spoon clattered against the sides of the cup as Bernie stirred milk and sugar into her tea. "It's just not fair. You come home exhausted every day, trying to work out the problems with the estate. Then there's that horrible Buckner woman who thinks she's entitled to money, as though a man's mistress has the same rights as a legal heir."

"She has a son, she claims is Farrell's. If the boy is my father's son, he should have rights to part of the estate. Leah Buckner won't believe me or my father's lawyer when we try to tell her there isn't any money. I suppose I can't blame her. She sees this big house and the Hart Corporation Building and translates them into dollar signs. She should count herself lucky Farrell deeded the condominium she lives in over to her, or it would be up on the chopping block with the rest of his property." Needing to find something positive about the situation, she added, "I got a good price for all three of Farrell's cars—the Ferrari, Mercedes, and Porsche—and an offer's been made on the boat. I accomplished that much this morning."

Then she'd returned to the Hart building only to run into reporters, photographers, and Nick.

"Try to forget her for now." Bernie said. "You've been working nonstop since you arrived. It's such a shame you had to give up your job in San Francisco in order to take care of your father's debts. It just isn't fair."

Tension tightened the muscles in Dionne's shoulders. "I didn't give up my job entirely, Bernie. I took a leave of absence. Another teacher is filling in for me." She didn't add that the woman substituting for her was due to have a baby in a month, which meant Dionne couldn't take forever to settle her father's affairs. The principal of the private school could decide it was more beneficial for the children if he hired a permanent teacher instead of a series of substitutes, leaving Dionne without a job.

Her classroom and her students felt very faraway at the moment. All the years of working to support herself and studying to get her teaching degree in special education seemed to have been accomplished by someone else. The difference between then and now was that then she had been able to see the end of the tunnel. Trying to unravel the financial disaster her father had left her only became more complicated as the days went by, with no end in sight.

She rubbed the back of her neck to try to ease the dull ache brought on by tension and stress. Exhaustion lay like a heavy weight on her shoulders, and she had to fight giving in to the need for sleep.

Before Bernie could offer more words of sympathy, Dionne forced her mouth to curve into a smile. "I believe I'll take a shower, Bernie. I'll be down in a while."

An hour later, dressed in a comfortable quilted lounging robe, Dionne helped Bernie serve the meal. Her father would have been horrified to see his daughter dining in such informal attire, which gave her a small sense of satisfaction. He wouldn't have been any happier about her taking her meals in the kitchen with the housekeeper, rather than alone in the formal dining room. Farrell Hart had been very big on appearances.

The old oval table Dionne and Bernie ate at was the one item of furniture Dionne was going to take back to her apartment in San Francisco. Years of wear marred its surface; several marks Dionne had made herself when she'd done her homework there while the cook prepared dinner. As Bernie served the roast Dionne traced the indentions she had made with a ballpoint pen years ago, her initials faded but still visible.

After dinner she brought out reams of computer readouts, studying them at the kitchen table until her eyes blurred. One of the properties she searched for was the abandoned school building Nick had been asking about. She discovered it was slotted for quick sale, since it would require extensive renovations before it could be used. She made a note to check with the accountant to see if donating the building and the land would help her tax liability. When she looked up the taxes, she saw they had been paid for the year, but were extremely high because of the location and size of the building. If she allowed the athletes to use the gymnasium for free, she would be operating at a loss.

Around midnight she climbed the curved stairs to the room she had occupied years ago. Even though her body was crying out for the oblivion of sleep, Dionne couldn't shut off her mind. Columns of figures she had been reading blurred with thoughts of Nick, making it impossible for her to block everything out.

Finally she dozed off, but the alarm rudely woke her before she was ready to face another day. She stayed longer than usual in the shower, yet it didn't help. She still felt groggy from lack of sleep, her movements sluggish as she pulled on a pair of gray sweatpants and yanked a gray sweatshirt over her head. Without bothering to brush her hair she tied it back with a ribbon, then shoved her feet into a pair of track shoes.

In front of the house she did a few stretching exercises, then ran down the driveway. Rather than leave the grounds, she continued jogging around the large circular drive. Each time she approached the gate, she checked to see if there were any reporters lurking outside. She saw no sign of them. After thirty minutes her sweatshirt was damp from perspiration and a blister was forming on the heel of her right foot.

She sat down on the grass to take off her shoe. After examining her heel she removed the other shoe. Carrying them, she started to walk back toward the house. Hearing a car coming up the drive, she turned to see who it was. The car looked very familiar. It should. It was hers.

Nick stopped the car when he came alongside her. Glancing at her shoes, he asked, "Did you blow a tire?"

"Very funny. What are you doing here, other than driving my car?"

"That's about it," he said casually. "I wouldn't turn down a cup of coffee."

"Neither would I." She pointed toward the front door. "You go ahead. I'm a little slower than the car. The door is unlocked. Bernie will give you some coffee if you go to the kitchen."

Nodding, he accelerated and parked in front of the house. Instead of going inside, though, he leaned against the car and crossed his arms over his chest.

Dionne didn't have to glance at him to know he was watching her. She could feel his intimate gaze flow over her, as though he were touching her. All he was doing was looking at her, and she was falling apart. Heaven help her when he really did touch her.

When she was within a few feet of him, she saw the now familiar fire in his dark eyes. He would touch her, she admitted to herself with resignation. And she would let him. It was as inevitable as the sunrise.

"I thought you didn't like sports," he said.

"I said I don't care for competing. Besides, this isn't sports. I run for exercise." Hoping she didn't sound as breathless as he was making her feel, she added, "I thought you wanted a cup of coffee. I doubt if Bernie will bring it out here."

"I was waiting for you."

She wished he wouldn't stare at her with such disturbing intensity. Especially since she must have looked like she'd been dragged through a swamp.

"You haven't stood on ceremony so far. Why now?"

He pushed away from the car and took the few steps that brought him to her. "I haven't said good morning."

His hand cupped the back of her neck and his mouth closed over hers gently. But there was nothing gentle about the jolt of pleasure shooting through her. All too soon he raised his head. "Good morning."

She slowly opened her eyes to meet his. The

possessive intimacy in his caress shook her as much as the passionate kiss they had exchanged before.

"Why are you doing this, Nick?" she asked quietly. "Every time I turn around, there you are. Touching me. Kissing me. Showing up at the oddest times for the oddest reasons. I've seen more of you the last couple of days than the whole time I lived here."

He raised his hand to brush damp tendrils of hair away from her face. "I'm not going to write about you, Dionne, but I plan on seeing more of you."

Her fingers wrapped around his wrist. "Maybe it's not what I want."

His expression serious, he slid his hand down her collarbone and brushed the back of his fingers over her breast, lingering on the hardening nipple. Her soft gasp brought his gaze back to hers.

He smiled slowly. "I think it is what you want."

She tightened her grip on his wrist to pull his hand away. "Sometimes we can't have what we want."

She turned away and ran up the steps. Wrenching open the front door, she left it ajar as she entered the house.

In her bedroom she yanked off her sweatshirt on her way to the bathroom. After she took another shower and blow-dried her hair, she dressed for work, choosing a taupe suit with a white silk blouse. Since the suit jacket had narrow black stripes running through it, she unearthed a pair of black heels and a small black purse. She brushed her hair back and arranged it in a twist that said more for neatness than fashion.

Examining herself in a floor-length mirror, she adjusted the lapel of the jacket. If she was going to stay much longer, she'd have to shop for some clothes. She had brought only enough for a week, and she'd already been there three. She was becoming heartily sick of wearing the same clothes over and over.

Before she went to the kitchen, she walked through the house and plugged in the phones. They remained blissfully silent. The only phone left to be reconnected was the one in the kitchen. As she approached the door she could hear Nick's deep masculine voice and Bernie's softer tones.

Inside the kitchen she saw Nick was sitting at the table across from Bernie, sharing a pot of coffee with her.

This morning he was wearing jeans and a print shirt under a casual waist-length jacket, which he had removed and draped over the back of his chair.

As soon as Dionne stepped into the room, Bernie hopped up from her chair. "If you'll excuse me, I have a few things to attend to in my room."

Dionne stared at Bernie as the older woman set her cup in the sink with a few other dishes. It was the first time Bernie hadn't insisted she eat a bountiful breakfast before she left the house. Dionne couldn't think of one single reason why

Bernie would be going to her room at this hour of the morning—except to leave her alone with Nicholas Lyon.

She sat down in the chair Bernie had occupied. Nick poured her a cup of coffee and pushed it across the table, along with the small pitcher of milk. It was an indication of how observant he was, since he obviously remembered she had poured cream into her coffee at Canaveri's.

As she stirred her coffee she looked at him, noting the tired lines around his eyes. "Have a rough night last night, Mr. Lyon? You look like you missed a few hours of sleep."

He smiled. "I did. It was your fault."

Refusing to be goaded, she replied, "If you're tired, why get up so early to bring my car to me? I was going to call a cab."

"That's your fault too."

She smiled slowly. "If I'm such a bad influence on you, why are you here?"

"I'd rather go crazy with you than go out of my mind thinking about you."

She knew the feeling. "What about your work?"

"I'll keep up with the deadlines." He poured himself another cup of coffee. "I got an idea for a column last night while I was thinking about you." He saw the wariness return to her eyes. "Don't worry. It's not about you, at least not directly. I started jotting down notes on walls."

"Blame it on the early hour, but I don't get the connection."

He leaned back in his chair. "There are all kinds

of walls. Tall ones, thick ones, long ones like the Great Wall of China. Some that come tumbling down like the Walls of Jericho. Then there are the walls you can't see, the solid ones people construct between themselves and other people."

"You might want to put in that people usually have reasons for building walls. If there weren't walls in a house, the roof would cave in."

"The walls don't have to come down if there was a door built into one, allowing others to come in," he said softly.

"And you're willing to sacrifice yourself as a taxi driver, so you can be the first one through the wall?"

Nick's eyes narrowed. Did she mean she had never allowed anyone close to her emotionally or physically? he wondered. He found it hard to believe she had never been with a man. She had to be twenty-nine years old, for pete's sake. Her response to his kisses hadn't been virginal by any means.

"I'm not the big bad wolf, Dionne. If you aren't comfortable thinking of me as a lover, try thinking of me as a friend. It's a start."

"I can always use another friend." She pushed her chair back. "I have to get some papers out of my bedroom. Then I'll be ready to go."

Nick draped an arm over the back of his chair as he watched her walk across the kitchen. She could have told him to take a flying leap. He wondered why she hadn't.

He found out when they were in the car.

"About tonight," she began as he drove through the gates of the estate. "If you had waited last night, I would have told you that I have too much work to take time off to go out."

"All the more reason for you to take a few hours off." He glanced at her. "Why do you have so much work to do? Are you planning on taking over your father's business?"

"No way," she said with a ghost of a laugh.

Well, he thought, that was clear enough. Not very helpful when he wanted to know the reason behind her decision, but clear. "So why do you have to spend every waking hour working for the Hart Corporation?"

"There is a lot to sort out before I can leave."

The part about her leaving wasn't what he wanted to hear. He didn't have much hope of her answering, but he asked anyway. "Where will you be going when you leave here?"

"San Francisco."

Feeling as though he were chiseling away at a boulder and coming up with grains of sand, he tried again. "Is there some reason why you have to return to San Francisco?"

"Yes."

His fingers tightened on the wheel. "Could you elaborate a little more?" he asked with a hint of irritation. "Like telling me why you have to leave Monterey to go to San Francisco. What's there that you can't have here?"

"Just my work, my friends, my home."

"What do you do?"

She didn't know why she was reluctant to tell him, except that it meant giving him more pieces of herself. "I teach children and adults with learning disabilities."

He jerked his head around to stare at her and almost ran into the car in front of him when the light turned red. He hit the brakes and told himself to do the same with his curiosity. "And you said I was full of surprises," he muttered. "I don't want to take away from what you do, but now you no longer have to work."

"Apparently you're under the same misconception that everyone else is, that because I'm Farrell Hart's heir, I must be rolling in it."

"It's a fair assumption to make, considering your father was one of the wealthiest men on the Peninsula." He gazed speculatively at her. "Are you saying your father didn't leave you everything?"

Dionne was thankful the light changed and Nick had to return his gaze to the road and the heavy traffic. "Farrell Hart left me everything," she answered honestly.

Nick was puzzled by the odd note in her voice, making her reply sound completely opposite of what she'd actually said. Something wasn't quite right, but he wasn't going to press her. At least not yet. There was something else he needed to know.

"It's occurred to me," he said quietly, "that you might have another reason you want to return to San Francisco."

She sighed, weary of the probing questions. "Does it make a difference what my reasons are?"

"It does if there's someone special waiting for you there."

She snapped her head around. "Why would that make any difference?"

"I like to know what I'm up against," he said, smiling at her.

"I'm not involved with anyone in San Francisco, not the way you mean. Which is the way I want it." She added for emphasis, "There or here."

"You're in for a big disappointment then."

As they approached the front of the Hart building, they were both relieved to see there were no picketers marching around in front, nor any sign of reporters.

"Does this mean you talked to the editor of the *Herald*?" Dionne asked.

He nodded. "I called him last night. He said he would make sure the reporters found something else to chase today." He didn't mention that Barry had said again that if there was a story connected with Dionne Hart, he expected Nick to find it.

He pulled into a parking spot behind his car, then got out to open her door for her. When she was standing beside him, she stared at the red car ahead of hers. "Nick, isn't that car like the one you drove when you were in high school?"

"It's not only just like it. It is the same car."

Her gaze flew to his face. "You're kidding."

He grinned. "A man never kids about his car, sweetheart."

She stepped over to the Mustang and ran her fingers lightly over the smooth rear fender. "I can't believe you still have the same car after all these years."

"When I find a good thing, I hang on to it." He locked her car and handed her the keys. "I'll see you tonight around seven-thirty."

"Nick, I really don't think it's a good idea to go out tonight. I meant what I said about having a lot of work to do."

He slipped his hand around to the back of her neck. "I meant what I said too. It won't hurt anything for you to take a few hours off."

She started to argue, but he stopped her effectively by covering her mouth with his own. He didn't care that they were on a public street. All that mattered was the feel of her mouth under his. His fingers tightened for a moment as his tongue sought hers. When he raised his head and saw the glazed look in her eyes, he had to fight the urge to pull her into his arms.

"Come with me tonight, Dionne."

This time he was giving her a choice, but after that kiss, she knew she really didn't have one. "I can't guarantee I can be finished by seven-thirty."

He didn't want to let her go, but he comforted himself with the knowledge that he would see her that night. He dropped his hand. "I'll wait for you."

She took several steps, then stopped. Turning slightly, she glanced back at him. "Are you going to be talking to your mother soon?"

"This afternoon. Why?"

"Will you tell her I hope she's feeling better?"

"Why don't you tell her yourself? I'm sure she would love to hear from you."

Her only reply was a small smile before she walked toward the building.

Nick remained by his car, watching her until she entered the building and was out of sight. He was admittedly not a patient man, but even he had to be satisfied with the progress he'd made with Dionne. She had actually agreed to go out with him, without him having to practically railroad her.

He slid behind the wheel of his car, then simply sat there. Already he was chafing at having to wait all day before he could see her again. He hoped Marty was happy his prediction had come true. Dionne Hart was definitely making him work to get close to her.

When he realized he was patting his empty pockets again, he stopped. A cigarette wouldn't help. He needed a large dose of patience.

Five

By five-thirty Dionne was feeling the effects of batting her head against a brick wall the entire day. All she'd accomplished was to get a pip of a headache.

Her first phone call informed her that the status of one of her pieces of property had changed from "maybe" to "no way." Another "sure thing" sale became "forget it" by nine-fifteen. Then the computer had a bad case of the hiccups and spat out disjointed data.

The day went from bad to worse. Her lawyer told her one of the businesses she'd thought was sold was filing for bankruptcy instead. Before lunch she had to sign papers that ultimately would put a hundred and twenty people out of work. The company didn't have the credit backing to purchase the site it leased, so the property had been sold to a conglomerate that was going to tear down the existing building and construct one of its own. She should be happy she could scratch two properties off her list. It was the way they had been disposed of that bothered her. It seemed that no matter what she did to rectify her father's mistakes, someone got hurt.

Yet, if she didn't sell all of Farrell's property, she would never be able to pay off the astounding debts on her own. Teacher's salaries did not rank high on the income scale.

The worst part of her day was when she learned one of the properties her father hadn't paid the taxes on was an address down by Cannery Row. The current tenants were Anissa and Paolo Canaveri. The realtor told Dionne that the Canaveris were attempting to come up with the money to buy the building, but it didn't look promising. The more publicized eating establishments at Cannery Row and Fisherman's Wharf drew the tourists. A small family restaurant located on a quiet side street wasn't a very good credit risk.

It was bad enough knowing her decisions affected people she didn't even know. Being responsible for Momma and Papa Canaveri losing their livelihood was too much. She asked the lawyer to look into forming an agreement whereby the Canaveris could apply their past leasing fees to the purchase of the property. Perhaps they could then get a loan for the lower amount, after the years of rental fees were deducted.

When she absorbed all the bad news she possibly could in one day, Dionne left the office. She was going to take advantage of the fact that she had two hours before Nick was due to pick her up. She would soak in a warm bath for at least an hour to try to relax before he arrived.

Then she saw a red Mustang parked in front of the house. She glanced at the clock on her dashboard to make sure she hadn't been wrong about the time. She hadn't been wrong. Nick was early. Two hours early.

She wasn't ready to see him yet, but it didn't look like she had a choice. The last thing she wanted to do was go to some sporting event, if that was what Nick still had planned. One thing she was learning about Nicholas Lyon was that he liked to do things his own way. Taking no for an answer wasn't exactly high on his list of things he did easily.

She drove around the side of the house and parked near the back door. When she entered the kitchen, she was startled to see Nick standing in front of the stove instead of Bernie. He was stirring something in a large pot with a big wooden spoon. A large white dish towel was folded and tied around his waist, apparently to protect his gray slacks. The sleeves of his gray-and-white-striped shirt were rolled up several turns. Next to him Bernie was peering into the pot.

Dionne asked the obvious question. "What's going on?"

Bernie leaned forward to see Dionne past Nick. "Oh, good. You're home early." Gesturing toward the large enamel pot, she explained, "Nick is show-ing me how to make killer chili."

Dionne stepped cautiously nearer to the stove and looked into the pot. The aroma made her eyes water. "Good Lord, Nick. Do you actually eat this or use it to strip paint off walls?"

Before he answered her, he cupped the back of her neck, a gesture she realized she was becom-ing dangerously used to. Tilting her head up to him, he kissed her briefly, an intimate greeting that set her heart to pounding.

Releasing her, he smiled, his eyes glittering with amusement and an erotic awareness. "You just wait until you try it. Your taste buds will thank you."

She removed a dab of the chili off his wooden spoon. Because it was so hot, she immediately stuck her finger in her mouth. It wasn't the heat of the chili that burned her tongue. The sauce was spicy and peppery, the flavor exploding in her mouth.

Nick was watching her with an expectant look in his eyes. "Well?"

When she got her breath back, she said truth-fully, "It's like nothing I've ever had before." She didn't add that she might never be able to taste anything ever again. Her tongue was numb.

Bernie shook her head in bemusement. "You should see all the ingredients he's put into the chili, Dionne. It's utterly amazing."

Dionne had nearly forgotten Bernie was there, but was grateful for her presence. Nick's continued scrutiny unnerved her. She had the feeling he saw more than she wanted him to see. Turning to Bernie, she said, "I'm not sure I want to know what's in that chili. Am I right in assuming we're having it for supper?"

Bernie chuckled. "I told Nick we were having a tuna casserole, and all of a sudden he started rummaging through the cupboards, saying he'd make his killer chili. I guess he doesn't care much for tuna casserole. I think on this auspicious occasion we should eat in the dining room."

Dionne dropped her purse on the table. "I think we should eat in here. It's closer to the fire extinguisher."

Nick set the spoon down. Dionne was trying to hide it, but he could tell she'd had a rough day. It was in her eyes and the rigid way she held herself, as though she were carrying a heavy load on her shoulders.

He walked over behind her and grasped her at the waist. She tensed instantly. "First," he said, "you're going to go get out of those clothes and into something more comfortable. Preferable a pair of tight jeans and a sexy sweater."

"I'm perfectly comfortable as I am." She resisted in vain as he turned her around and urged her out of the kitchen.

"But you're still in your business duds. I don't want anything to remind you of work tonight."

When they reached the bottom of the stairs, he stopped. It was as far as he'd go. Accompanying her to her bedroom was a temptation he didn't feel strong enough to resist. The subtle swaying of her hips beneath his hands as he had marched her out of the kitchen was mind-blowing enough. It had made him think of how her lower body would feel under his, rubbing against him as he made love to her.

Dionne hesitated when he dropped his hands and clearly expected her to go upstairs. "Did I get the time wrong?" she said. "Didn't you say you were coming around seven-thirty?"

"That was then." He'd spent all morning and afternoon thinking about her instead of working on his column. About an hour ago he'd given up and driven to the house, feeling like a lovesick adolescent. "It occurred to me you might want to eat something before we go to the arena."

She leaned her hip against the banister. "So you came up with killer chili. I think I'd feel safer with the tuna casserole."

The flowery scent of her perfume drifted around him, clouding his judgment. "You'll have to trust me. The chili isn't actually lethal."

"That's comforting."

"That isn't easy for you, is it?" he said seriously. When she frowned in puzzlement, he added, "Trusting someone."

Dionne was beginning to feel as if she were still in low gear and he had already shifted into overdrive. "Is it important to trust the cook before you sample his dish?"

"It helps." Giving in to the need to touch her, to comfort her as well as himself, he stroked the soft skin just below her ear. "Have a bad day at the office?"

Her smile was a little ragged around the edges, but it was the best she could manage. "I've had better."

"Well, your workday is officially over." He leaned forward and touched her lips with his. "Hurry and change before the chili eats a hole in the pan."

All day she had been in one losing battle after the other, and she didn't have any fight left. "Okay," she murmured, turning to go up the stairs.

"Dionne?"

Stopping on the third step, she looked down at him. "What?"

He was going to ask her what was troubling her, but he changed his mind. She was worn out. It wasn't a good time to give her the third degree. Or take her out when she would prefer not to go.

"Dionne, I've changed my mind. I'm being self-ish by forcing you to do something you would obviously rather not do."

Part of her wanted to take him up on his offer not to go. She couldn't understand why she found herself saying, "I've changed my mind too. I want to go."

"Are you sure?"

"No, but I'm going."

"I meant what I said about jeans. They'll be more appropriate for where we're going than a suit or a dress."

"Jeans," she muttered. "Right." She continued

to gaze at him for a few seconds more, waiting to see if he had anything else to say. When he simply stared back at her, his eyes fathomless with emotion, she continued up the stairs.

Nick watched Dionne until she disappeared out of sight. Then, instead of returning to the kitchen to wait for her, he sat down on the third step.

When he had talked to his mother earlier, he should have asked if there were any mentally deranged members of the family he didn't know about. If not, he might qualify as the first. Dionne confused him, tantalized him, irritated him, and intrigued him as no woman had before. No matter how many obstacles she threw up between them, he was determined to tear them down. He knew the barriers were there. What he didn't know was why she felt she needed them.

And why he was so intent on getting past them.

His mother hadn't been much help when he'd asked her about Dionne. It was obvious from things Dionne had let slip that his mother had known her better than he'd originally thought. However, after her initial shock at learning that her son's interest in Dionne wasn't mild curiosity, Blanche had been adamant about respecting Dionne's confidences. A reserved person herself, Blanche could understand Dionne's wish for privacy.

So, instead of answering his questions, she asked one of her own. "Why the sudden interest in Dionne Hart, Nick? It had better not be for an article you're writing. I doubt if Dionne has changed that much that she is seeking publicity."

He heard the warning in her voice and attempted to clarify his interest. It was basically what he'd said to Dionne. "I'm interested in her, not who she is. There's so much I don't know about her and she's certainly not a wellspring of information. I would get more from a prisoner of war than she volunteers, and all they give is name, rank, and serial number."

His mother's soft chuckle came over the line. "Trophies aren't awarded until the end of the race. Be patient for once in your life, Nick."

It wasn't that he had a choice, he thought with irritation. Realizing he was an inch short of sulking, he pushed himself up off the stair and strode into the kitchen to wait for Dionne.

It took Dionne fifteen minutes to change—five minutes to take a shower, six minutes to unearth a pair of white jeans, and four minutes to put them on and a white shirt. Because she was too tired to fuss with her hair, she brushed it and ignored it.

Downstairs she joined Nick and Bernie in the kitchen. Like Dionne, Nick had turned down the housekeeper's suggestion that they eat in the formal dining room.

As they ate the chili, Nick kept them laughing with various amusing stories, some apparently true, some stretched to the limit of believability, which made them even funnier. Several times Bernie had to use her napkin to dab at her eyes.

Dionne, too, forgot her problems and enjoyed his nonsense.

Which was exactly what Nick had hoped to accomplish. Dionne wasn't eating as much as he would have liked, and he didn't think it was because she didn't like the chili. Whatever had happened during the day had receded in her mind, but still hovered in the background.

Bernie contributed to the conversation by relating a few incidents from Dionne's childhood. Nick noticed Farrell Hart didn't figure in any of the episodes. Most took place in the kitchen, like the time Dionne attempted to cook by combining all the ingredients she could reach on the first shelf of a cupboard, ending with an indescribable glop.

"You enjoyed that, didn't you?" Dionne said later as she and Nick drove away from the house. "When Bernie was telling you about me picking the flowers the gardener had just planted, you nearly fell off your chair laughing."

"Bernie showed me a side of you I hadn't seen before. Of course I enjoyed it."

"Is that why we're going to a sports event? So you can see another side of me?"

He grinned at her. "No. Tonight is just for fun. I don't think you've had much fun, Dionne. That's going to change."

The sporting event Nick took her to was a track-and-field competition held at the Carmel High School football field, for youngsters trying out for the Special Olympics.

The bleachers were packed when they arrived.

There were no reserved seats, but Nick found them a place in the middle of a row about halfway up. Once they were seated, Dionne was overly conscious of his hip and thigh pressed against hers. And several times she had to quell the urge to move closer.

After a few minutes he took a bunched up bag out of his jacket pocket and handed it to her. Opening it up, she peeked inside and saw that Nick had kept his word. He had brought her caramel corn.

She wasn't sure what the combination of chili and caramel corn would do to her stomach, but she thanked him anyway.

A number of events were going on at the same time, which made it difficult for Dionne to watch everything at once. She was amused at one point to see an older woman in the row ahead of her peacefully knitting away as she watched the competitions on the field. Everyone else was a bit more enthusiastic, clapping and yelling encouragement to the various participants. Every child received huge applause whether they won or lost, their smiles ample reward for the crowd's enthusiasm.

Rather than try to watch everything at once, Dionne concentrated on the track event about to begin directly in front of them. It was a fifty-meter race, and six young boys were jumping up and down in their eagerness to get going. Watching them, she remembered being a volunteer at her first Special Olympics in San Francisco. There had been enough volunteers for each child to have his own "hugger," and it was one of the most satisfying things Dionne had ever done.

Whether her child or any of the other children finished an event, they were hugged. To Dionne the embraces were more valuable than any trophy, medal, or ribbon could be. The accolade of affection was a prize she'd been willing to bestow, receiving as much as the children.

Seeing the earnest faces of the young people as they put everything they had into each race, each jump, each hurdle, made Dionne ashamed of the self-pity she had been wallowing in all day. Instead of feeling sorry for herself, she should be applying every ounce of her energy into finding the solutions.

After they had been there about an hour, Nick astonished her by asking if she wanted anything to eat. He was going to go get a hot dog.

"You've got to be kidding," she said. "You just had two bowls of chili for dinner. How can you possibly be hungry?"

"It's like popcorn at a movie. You have to have a hot dog at a sporting event. It's an unwritten law."

She laughed. "You go ahead, but I'll pass."

He removed his jacket and handed it to her to hold. She folded it onto her lap and watched as he worked his way down the row to the steps. He excused himself again and again, making jokes and comments to the people he was disturbing. One thing hadn't changed about Nick, Dionne

IT'S EASY TO ENTER BANTAM BOOKS' DREAM MAKER SWEEPSTAKES!

Where will Passion lead you?

CARIBBEAN   EUROPE   HAWAII

YOU'RE INVITED

to enter our Dream Maker Sweepstakes for a chance to win a romantic 14-day vacation for two to Hawaii, Europe or the Caribbean...PLUS, you can win *$1,000 Cash*...or a 27" RCA Color TV!

Don't break our heart!

Peel off both halves of this heart and unite them on the Entry Form enclosed. Use both halves to get the most from this special offer.

FREE ENTRY! FREE BOOKS!

SPECIAL BONUS:

Get 6 FREE Loveswept books, *plus* another wonderful gift just for trying Loveswept Romances. See details inside...

DON'T HOLD BACK!

1. **No obligation!** No purchase necessary! Enter our Sweepstakes for a chance to win!
2. **FREE!** Get your first shipment of 6 Loveswept books *and* a lighted makeup case as a free gift.
3. **Save money!** Become a member and every month you get 6 books for the price of 5! Return any shipment you don't want.
4. **Be the first!** You'll always receive your Loveswept books before they are available in stores. You'll be the first to thrill to these exciting new stories.

Detach here and mail today.

BANTAM BOOKS' DREAM MAKER SWEEPSTAKES

Entry Form

YES! I want to see where passion will lead me!

Place FREE ENTRY Sticker Here

Place FREE BOOKS Sticker Here

Enter me in the sweepstakes! I have placed my **FREE ENTRY** sticker on the heart.

Send me six *free* Loveswept novels *and* my *free* lighted makeup case! I have placed my **FREE BOOKS** sticker on the heart.

Mend a broken heart. Use both stickers to get the most from this special offer!

10355

NAME _____

ADDRESS _____ APT _____

CITY _____

STATE _____ ZIP _____

Loveswept's Heartfelt Promise to You!

There's no purchase necessary to enter the sweepstakes. There is no obligation to buy when you send for your free books and lighted makeup case. You may preview each new shipment for 15 days free. If you decide against it, simply return the shipment within 15 days and owe nothing. If you keep them, pay only $2.09 per book — a savings of 41¢ per book (plus postage, handling, and sales tax in NY and IL.)

Prices subject to change. Orders subject to approval.
See complete sweepstakes rules at the back of this book. **BR23**

Give in to love and see where passion leads you!
Enter the Dream Maker Sweepstakes and send
for your FREE lighted makeup case and 6
FREE Loveswept books today!
(See details inside.)

mused. His mother had once told her that ever since he was a small boy, Nick could talk to a tree and get a response. Seeing him now, she believed it.

She also noticed the glances he received from several women, and she could understand why he attracted their gazes. It wasn't just his looks. No one had to tell her about the natural grace in his walk or the way his smile could melt the coldest iceberg.

The trip back to his seat was a little trickier for Nick since he was balancing two hot dogs and two cold drinks in a flimsy cardboard box. Several people laughed as he feigned spilling the food when he stepped past them.

Dionne was so engrossed in trying to watch all of the events on the field, she didn't even notice when Nick held his hot dog out to her and she took a bite.

He chuckled. "Are you enjoying yourself?"

She had to wait a moment until she finished chewing. "I like watching the kids have fun." She glanced at him. "I can see that they're having a great time, but I can't help wondering if there isn't a better way than teaching them to compete with each other."

"Participating in sports isn't just competing, Dionne. It isn't just winning and losing. These kids are learning teamwork and sportsmanship in a way that's fun and challenging. What's wrong with that?"

"Anytime there's a winner, there has to be a

loser. It's great for the one who wins but hard on the one who loses. To some children the pressure to compete, to win, can be devastating, especially if they aren't particularly coordinated."

He studied her. "You claim not to like sports at all, yet you just said you were enjoying yourself."

"I've never said I don't like sports. I just don't think competitive games are as important as you seem to think they are. Instead of pushing children so much toward competing, I would like to see some of them directed toward the arts." Noting his skeptical expression, she continued, "What are prized and treasured in museums, valuable beyond price? A football or a painting like the 'Mona Lisa'?"

Nick choked back a laugh. "What about suits of armor? They were worn in jousting contests, which were a sport at one time. They're in museums too."

"They were designed mainly for battle, not sports."

"I see I have my work cut out for me, trying to show you the benefits of competing in sports."

"You just contradicted yourself," she said smugly. "You claim it's not just competing."

They were so engrossed in their argument, neither of them noticed the race down on the track. Those around them did. A loud cheer went up with everyone getting to their feet when the relay race ended. The man behind Dionne forgot he had a large cup full of cola between his knees. When he stood up, the contents spilled over

Dionne's back and shoulders, and down the front of her shirt.

When the cold drink hit her, the bag of caramel corn went flying as Dionne jumped to her feet. Nick grabbed her before she toppled over onto the people below.

"I'm terribly sorry," the man behind her said, bending down. "Are you all right, miss?"

She smiled wanly at the man. "I'm fine." A piece of ice slid down her back, and she shivered. "Accidents happen."

Nick started brushing off the chips of ice that stuck to her clothing. She had left her suede jacket in the car, and the soda had soaked her thin blouse, making it nearly transparent. His gaze was drawn to her breasts, her nipples clearly visible against the wet cloth.

"Put this on," he ordered, picking his jacket up.

When she had it on, he zipped it up to make sure she was completely covered. "I'll take you home."

The man who had spilled the drink apologized again, but Nick cut him off. Holding her arm, he mumbled his excuses again as he led Dionne down the row. Once they were on the steps, he clasped her hand and headed for the exit.

When they reached his car, she started to take off his jacket, but he stopped her. "Leave it on."

"I suppose I'd better. Otherwise I'll get your car as sticky as I've gotten your jacket."

"That isn't why."

Startled by his harsh tone, she stared curiously

at him. "It really wasn't that man's fault, Nick. He didn't do it on purpose."

"I know." He unzipped the jacket and pushed the sides back. Once more he couldn't resist staring at her breasts. "This jacket is the only thing keeping me from taking your shirt off," he said hoarsely, lifting his gaze to hers. "Even with your shirt on, you're practically naked. If we weren't in a public place, I'd be tempted to lick that cola from your breasts. Hell," he muttered, "I'm tempted anyway."

Her eyes widened in shock. She peeked at her breasts and saw what he meant. Then she looked up at him. Desire flared in his eyes, sending heat streaking through her.

"Nick," she said softly, yearningly.

He smiled. "I know. This isn't the time or the place." He touched her hair. "But soon there will be the right time and the right place, Dionne. I want you very much. You could be covered in mud and I would still want you."

She didn't resist when he drew her closer. She couldn't. When he kissed her, it was like the first time, yet different in a way she couldn't begin to describe. Tenderness blended with passion as he parted her lips to deepen the caress.

She sank into the oblivion of need as he held her tighter, his tongue stroking hers. They were close, yet not close enough. They were intimate, yet not intimate enough. They were approaching the point of no return, with desire leading them.

His large jacket fell off her shoulders when she

slid her arms around his neck. Her wet shirt stained the front of his. Neither noticed or cared. Passion had heightened their need and lowered their resistance.

Nick felt her shiver against him, and didn't know if it was due to his caresses or because she was cold. In case it was the latter, he reluctantly released her and pulled the jacket back up over her shoulders. Wrapping it around her again, he held on to the zippered front.

"I don't want to take you back to the estate," he said.

"I can't very well go anyplace else like this."

He almost suggested they go to his ranch, but bit back the words. They still had a lot of ground to cover before they could reach their final destination.

Six

When he parked the car in front of the estate, Nick
didn't give Dionne a chance to brush him off at
the door. He took her keys from her and unlocked
the door. "I wouldn't turn down a cup of coffee,"
he said, handing the keys back to her.

Dionne hesitated for a moment. The blood was
still racing in her veins. Desire still blazed in his
eyes. If he came in, he would demand more from
her than coffee. She turned the knob and pushed
open the door.

"Bernie's probably in her room at this hour,"
she said, and gestured toward the kitchen. "If you
don't mind starting the coffee, I'll go change into
something less sticky. She keeps the grounds in
the refrigerator."

Nick stayed where he was as she walked up the
stairs, enjoying the tantalizing view of her swaying

hips. When she reached the landing, she paused and looked down at him. Their gazes held for a few seconds, then she smiled slightly and continued on to her bedroom.

If she were alone, she would simply put on her comfortable old robe. But she wasn't alone. Nick was waiting for her. She exchanged her cola-stained shirt for an oversized black one. When she returned to the first floor, she started toward the kitchen until she heard him call her from the living room.

Changing direction, she walked into the living room and found Nick sitting on the couch, leaning against the Spanish shawl she had spread across the back of it. The shawl had once decorated a grand piano, but she had sold it. She would take the shawl with her when she returned to San Francisco.

As soon as he saw her in the doorway, Nick sat forward and poured her a cup of coffee. He'd set a tray containing a decanter of coffee, two cups, and a pitcher of milk on the low mahogany table in front of the couch. As he added milk to her cup, he muttered something she didn't catch. She could see he was frowning though.

"Why are you frowning?" she asked, sitting down beside him.

He glanced at her shirt. "I've been giving myself a hard lecture the whole time you were upstairs, and it wasn't even necessary."

"What kind of lecture?"

"I told myself that if you came down wearing a

sexy robe, I was to keep my hands off you. At least until we've talked." He plucked at the sleeve of her shirt. "It doesn't make any difference what you're wearing. In coveralls or a business suit, I still want you so bad I ache."

She curled one leg under her, shifting sideways to look at him. "Nick, I'm not sure—"

"That's all right. I'm sure enough for both of us." He leaned back again and stared at a spot on the wall opposite them. "What's going on, Dionne?"

It was her turn to frown. "I told you before, Nick. I didn't come back to Monterey to get involved with anyone."

"That isn't what I meant. I know what's going on with us. I want to know what's going on around you. I've been in this house a few times when your father was having one of his charity affairs. I remember this room in particular. It was overflowing with valuable antiques, and there were several paintings on the walls that aren't there now. There were also a squadron of maids and a butler who served wine and dainty little sandwiches. The antiques are gone. There are blank spots on the walls where the paintings hung. The only member of the staff I've seen is Bernie. You were trying to fix the fountain instead of leaving it to the gardener or a handyman. Your father had to have had both since I can't see him mowing the lawn or changing a light bulb himself. Why are you selling everything?"

She played with the fringe of the shawl. "I don't have the same priorities my father had."

Nick tamped down his temper before it flared up. In the art of evasive fencing she was a master. And it was beginning to irritate the hell out of him. "I'm glad to hear it." He switched his own priorities. "I can also remember what you were wearing when you asked me to come to your birthday party. You had on a brown skirt and a rust-colored sweater that was two sizes too big for you. You held three schoolbooks clenched to your chest like armor. An English lit book, a loose-leaf notebook, and an American history text." Pausing briefly, he added, "When I turned down your invitation, you looked like I'd just slapped you."

She was silent for a long moment, feeling sorry for that young girl, yet also relieved she was no longer that defenseless.

"Why bring that up now?" she asked.

"To get it out of the way."

This time she didn't evade him or the subject. "I had a terrible crush on you," she admitted, smiling.

"So did I."

To her amazement she found herself laughing. "You were fairly arrogant. That was probably part of the attraction. The captain of the football team, senior class president, the apple of your mother's eye, and you drove a flashy red Mustang. You were the hero of every girl in the sophomore class. Me included." She paused for a moment, then added, "Did you know it was your mother who suggested I have a birthday party? And that I invite you to come?"

He was as surprised by what she said as by her actually saying it. He was getting more than he had expected. "My mother? Why?"

"Apparently Bernie mentioned my birthday was coming up and that I'd never had a birthday party that she could remember. Your mother was horrified and set out to change that."

He smiled with affection. "She's always been very big on birthdays. Still is. Even with a broken hip, she engineered a birthday party for me in her hospital room a few weeks ago. There was a cake, balloons, and even a few nurses wearing party hats. After my father died when I was six, she still managed to make a celebration out of my birthday, even though there wasn't much money. It might have been only a cupcake with a candle in it and a small gift, but she made it a special day."

"I hope you appreciate the fact that you have an exceptional mother."

"I do." He reached out and took her hand, spreading her fingers to lace them through his own. "She's hoping to see you when she returns home. I told her we might drive down to see her."

Dionne stared down at their clasped hands rather than meet his gaze. "I doubt if I'll have the time. There's still a lot to do to settle my father's estate."

He glanced around the room. "Which brings us back to the question I asked a while ago that you haven't answered."

She shrugged. "I've sold a few things."

"I already figured that out. Why?"

She pulled her hand away from his and started to stand, but he stopped her with his voice. "No more evasions, Dionne. If there is a problem, maybe I can help you with it."

"Is this offer from Nicholas Lyon the man or Nicholas Lyon the journalist?"

His eyes flashed gold fire. If he touched her, it would be in anger, and he wouldn't do that. He sprang off the couch and put some distance between them. With his hands clamped to his hips he faced her from the other side of the table. "Dammit, Dionne. You don't make it easy for anyone to get close to you. I'll be damned if you're going to use my occupation as a barrier between us. I'm offering to help you because I care about you, not because I'm doing research for an article. If you don't know that I'm not the type of man to use people for my own gain, then you have the perception of a gnat."

She could have continued arming her defenses. Instead she told him what he wanted to know because he had said he cared about her. It was that simple.

"My father's estate isn't quite as healthy as everyone thinks it is."

He stared at her. A large chunk of the wall she'd put up had tumbled down. Exultation ran through him in shock waves. Having breached the wall, he didn't push for details. They would have to come from her when she was ready. Otherwise they wouldn't mean as much.

"What can I do to help?"

His question stunned her. He wasn't going to press for more information, but simply offered to help. Because of that, she went one step further. "I'm not the one that needs help. It's the people who have leased my father's property that need help. Everything has to be sold to pay off his debts. Some of the businesses have made arrangements to buy the property, but there are others who can't afford to." She paused, and regret and guilt mingled in her voice when she continued. "Like the Canaveris."

Nick slowly returned to the couch and sat down beside her. Once again, she'd given him far more than he'd expected. "I took it for granted they owned the restaurant."

"My father was possessive about what he owned. From what I can gather, various businesses wanted to purchase the properties they were leasing after they had become established, but my father kept renewing leases rather than selling outright. Now the selling price is compounded by the fact that Farrell didn't pay property taxes on any of the land for the past year."

Nick's lips pursed as he whistled silently. "And I badgered you about the school building gymnasium. Like everyone else, I thought Farrell had left you everything on a gold platter."

"I want people to think exactly that. If it gets around that I'm desperate to sell, I won't be able to get the asking price."

While absorbing what she had told him, Nick also realized she was trusting him with information that could harm her if it leaked out. The extent of her trust stunned him.

She was being open with him, exposing parts of her life for the first time. Her vulnerability attracted him more than her beauty ever had. She hid it well, but now he had uncovered it. He wondered if she realized what she was giving him. Or if she would ever come to regret it. Not if he could help it.

"It's not your fault if the Canaveris or others are in a difficult situation. Your father caused it, not you."

"It's my responsibility now. If I make the wrong decision, people like the Canaveris can be ruined financially."

He reached for her, ignoring her gasp of surprise as he lifted her onto his lap. "There's nothing you can do tonight. There's always tomorrow."

She gave him a half-smile as she relaxed against his chest. It was advice she was more than willing to take. "What should I think of instead?"

"Me."

His lips skimmed her throat, teasing and tasting. She shivered under the onslaught of erotic sensations, but she didn't draw away. The world of sensuality he had introduced her to opened up again, and she clutched him to make sure she wasn't alone. She felt his warm, hard mouth on her jawline, her cheeks, her eyes. Everywhere but on her lips.

Thrusting her fingers into his hair, she brought his mouth to hers. He made a soft, low sound deep in his throat as she initiated a closer intimacy. Blood surged through his body, hot and searing as his tongue plunged into her mouth to mate with hers. She met him with honest passion, without any fear or resistance.

The feel of her hand on his bare skin made him aware she had unbuttoned his shirt. Needing to feel her flesh, too, he swiftly unfastened the buttons on her shirt. His mind spun as he pushed the shirt aside to reveal her creamy breasts. When she had changed her clothes earlier, she had only put on the shirt.

Raising his head to see her eyes, he slid his hand across her rib cage to cup one breast.

When she closed her eyes, he murmured, "No. Look at me. I want to see how you like the feel of my hands."

Lifting her lashes slowly, she met his hot gaze. He saw his own need and desire reflected in the depths of her eyes.

Before easing her down onto the cushions, Nick swept away her shirt, then his own. Half-covering her body as he sprawled out beside her, he bent his head to taste the tempting swell of her breast, lingering over the hard nipple. Her hips undulated against his as she instinctively sought his aroused body.

Nick thought he would explode if he didn't bury himself deep inside her soon. There was pleasure in touching her, feeling her tongue stroking his, but it wasn't enough. Not nearly enough.

His fingers found the snap of her jeans. Sliding

the zipper down, he followed it with his hand, slipping under the cool fabric of her panties to find the core of her femininity. She arched up to him as he took her up and over the wall of desire.

As though from a long distance, he heard Dionne murmur his name. She reached for him, her arms wrapping around him when he claimed her mouth once more. Reality faded as desire exploded.

Dionne felt the rough material of her jeans sliding down her legs. The air cooled her heated skin only briefly, then Nick's fiery touch flowed over her, searing her flesh and heating her blood. She pressed her thighs together in an attempt to ease the empty ache between them, assuaged only slightly by the rhythmic thrust of his tongue against hers.

In a far corner of her mind a realization grew stronger until she could no longer ignore it.

"Nick, we have to stop," she said huskily.

He wasn't sure he could. It was the last thing he wanted to do, especially with her nearly naked body pressed against his.

"Why?"

"Bernie. She's in her room, but she could come out at any time." Aching regret deepened her voice. "This can't be the time or the place."

He drew air into his lungs to try to steady his thudding heart. Allowing himself one long last look at her tempting body, he reached behind him for the Spanish shawl. As he sat up he drew her with him, draping the shawl around her.

For a moment he rested his forearms on his

thighs, closing his eyes against the burning ache in his loins. Her scent and taste were everywhere, on his hands, his lips, tempting him, tantalizing him, driving him mad with a desperate need.

He knew she was right. This wasn't the time or the place. When they did finally make love, he wanted privacy without the threat of any interruptions. For a long, long time.

He heard her moving, then felt the cushion give slightly as she swung her legs to the floor and sat up. Not trusting himself to look at her, he reached for the cup of coffee he had poured earlier. It was stone cold, but he drank every drop without a grimace.

Setting the cup back down, he got to his feet. Without looking at her, he murmured. "I'll call you tomorrow."

Dionne sat numbly on the couch and watched him walk out of the room. Suddenly she clenched the shawl around her naked breasts and ran after him.

"Nick, wait."

He stopped several feet from the door, but he didn't face her. "Don't let me touch you again, Dionne. I'm barely hanging on as it is."

Her bare feet made no sound as she approached him. "I'm sorry, Nick. This isn't how I wanted the evening to end either."

He finally turned around. "You keep thinking everything is your fault, Dionne. I was the one stripping your clothes off and enjoying every moment of it."

She heard the strain in his voice and understood it. She was feeling it too. The need to touch him again was overwhelming, and she gave in to it. But she got more than she bargained when she lightly stroked his forearm.

He grabbed her upper arms and whirled her around, pressing her back against the door. The shawl fell off her shoulders, exposing the soft rise of her breasts to his avid gaze. He sucked in his breath. "I told you not to touch me, Dionne. I've always considered myself a strong man, but you make me weak."

The raw hunger in his voice was nothing compared to the blatant sensuality of his kiss. As his tongue plunged into her mouth he leaned his lower body into hers, grinding against her. She made a sound of torment mixed with pleasure, and it nearly sent him over the edge.

Releasing her, he placed his hands on the door on either side of her head. Slowly, regretfully, he moved his hips back so their bodies were no longer touching. It would have been easier to cut off an arm.

"Dionne, I have to go or I'll end up taking you right here in the foyer."

She nodded. Drawing the shawl back around her, she folded her arms in front of her. She was shaking like the last leaf on a tree during a winter storm, but she couldn't help it.

He backed up and waited for her to move away. When she finally stepped aside, he opened the door. Just before he left, he allowed himself one last look. The black fringe of the shawl brushed against her bare thighs. Her honey-blond hair was mussed from his fingers, her lips swollen from his kisses.

Doing the honorable thing wasn't half as tempting as saying to hell with it. Still, he murmured quietly, "Good night, Dionne."

He left.

Seven

Unlike the previous Saturdays since she'd been
back in Monterey, Dionne didn't bother reading
the computer readouts with their endless columns
of ominous figures. At this point there was little
she could do. All the offers had been made. It was
now up to the realtors, the lawyers, the bankers,
and the prospective buyers.

She could only wait, and she was finding that
the hardest part. It occurred to her that she could
wait in San Francisco, leaving everything in the
hands of the professionals. Except that would mean
leaving Nick.

After breakfast Bernie announced she was going
to start packing some of her belongings, refusing
Dionne's offer of assistance. Too restless just to
sit around, Dionne decided to tackle a job she'd
been putting off for too long. She had gone through

the entire house, room by room, making lists of the remaining items that were to go to various antique dealers and auction houses. In another week the house would be completely empty.

She had avoided one room. Her father's study. When she was a child it was one of two rooms she had been forbidden to enter. Farrell's bedroom was the other. The housekeeper and his mistresses had been allowed to cross the threshold of his bedroom, and the housekeeping staff and his business associates were invited into his sanctum. His daughter was not.

Except for the night before she had left Monterey.

As she put the key in the lock, Dionne pushed all thoughts of that night from her mind. It took her two attempts to unlock the door. If her hand hadn't been shaking so much, she might have managed the first time. The air was musty and stale, but the furniture was free of dust, which attested to Bernie's rigid housekeeping standards. When Dionne flicked the switch near the door, several lamps went on around the room. Her gaze was drawn to the glass-enclosed case built along one wall. Trophies adorned the shelves. They were backlit by lights and reflected in mirrors, making it appear as though there were twice as many as there actually were.

The floor-to-ceiling bookcases were filled with leather-bound books she doubted if her father had ever opened. Like everything else in the house, they were probably for show. The top of the large antique desk was completely bare except for an ornate brass inkwell and pen set. Several hunting prints hung on the wall opposite the desk, a dark red leather couch beneath them.

All she had noticed that night fourteen years ago was her father and the trophies he had thrust in her face one by one, for her to read the inscriptions. Now she saw the room wasn't as big as she'd thought. It wasn't as overburdened with opulence as the rest of the house, but the dark green carpet and heavy furniture didn't exactly make for a cheerful, homey environment.

After carting many cardboard boxes into the room, Dionne walked around the desk and pushed the high-back leather chair to one side. She certainly wasn't going to sit in it. All of the desk drawers were locked, though, and she was momentarily stymied. Then she remembered her father had taken a small key out of the inkwell to open the top right-hand drawer the night she had been summoned to his study. The drawer that had contained her passport. The key was still there.   •

An hour later when Nick stepped into the room and looked around, he thought Bernie had been mistaken when she told him Dionne was in Farrell Hart's study. All he could see were stacks of papers piled on top of the desk and overflowing a wastebasket. The glass doors to a lighted case built into the wall were open, the shelves empty.

The sound of paper rustling behind the desk finally told him where she was.

He had to step over several boxes as he made

his way across the room. Dressed in jeans and a white T-shirt, Dionne was sitting cross-legged on the floor, a square tin box in front of her. She was staring at something in her hand.

When he spoke her name, she looked up. He saw the glint of sensual awareness in her eyes, but she didn't smile. He didn't need to ask what she was doing. She was clearing out her father's things. And she wasn't enjoying it.

Moving a box out of his way, he sat down beside her. "Need any help?"

She shook her head. "There are a few papers I'll turn over to my father's attorney and let him worry about what to do with them. Otherwise the rest can be thrown away."

His gaze was drawn to the item she still held in her hand. It was a passport.

He took it from her and opened it. Inside he saw a black-and-white photo of a younger Dionne, the shy teenager who had asked him to her six-teenth birthday party. He turned several pages, but they were blank. The passport had never been used.

"And this?" he asked.

She grabbed it out of his hand and tossed it into the wastebasket. "That's where it should have been years ago," she said with satisfaction.

He leaned against the bookcase behind him, drawing his knees up and resting his wrists on them. "It's never been used. Why did your father keep it?"

"That's a good question." Her mouth twisted slightly. "Maybe as a souvenir."

"Odd sort of souvenir."

That was exactly what she had thought when she'd found it in the tin box. It was the last thing she had expected her father to keep. But the passport wasn't the only surprising thing she had found.

She took a thick sheaf of papers from the box and held them up. "I found these too. They're reports from his lawyer dating from about three months after I left Monterey to the present day in six-month increments. A number of different private detectives were hired to keep tabs on my whereabouts." She shook her head. "Farrell knew where I was the whole time."

Nick glanced at the papers. He would like to have taken a look at those reports, but he wasn't going to ask to see them. Giving her father the benefit of the doubt, he murmured, "Maybe it was because he cared."

She looked up. "Maybe, but I don't think so. Also in the reports are accounts of my mother's affairs until she died, and I'm not talking about social events like sherry and cheese parties."

"When did your mother die?"

"When I was ten."

"Did you ever see her after she left Monterey?"

"No. I never heard from her. She did leave me a trust fund, however, which meant she either remembered she had a daughter or she couldn't think of anyone else to leave her money to."

Nick wasn't surprised by her mother's actions or Dionne's attitude. He might have been at one time, but not any longer.

"Obviously," he said, "you weren't disappointed when you weren't allowed to go with your mother when your parents divorced."

She shrugged. "I never saw her much when she lived with my father, so I barely noticed when she left."

She'd had parents without actually having parents, he thought. It was unbelievable.

"I have a question for you," she said, as she placed the contents back in the box. "What are you doing here?"

He smiled crookedly. "You already know the answer."

She did. Even if he wasn't looking at her with fire in the depths of his dark eyes, she knew.

He slid his arm around her and pulled her back to lean against him. "Tell me about the passport."

Dionne told herself it was ridiculous to be upset about the passport or the reports that proved she hadn't really gotten away from her father after all. When she left Monterey, she had pushed the memory of the night he had shown her the passport far back in her mind. Now Nick was asking her to bring it out into the open. Maybe it was time, she mused. And maybe Nick was the one she should tell. The night before they had crossed an invisible line, and it would be difficult to go back. Maybe impossible. She realized she no longer wanted to.

She took a deep breath and relaxed against him,

her head on his shoulder. "I was supposed to use the passport to go live with my maternal grand-mother in England. I didn't go."

Nick tilted his head forward and to one side so he could see her face. "When was this?"

"Two weeks after my sixteenth birthday."

He stroked her arm. He wasn't sure whether it was to soothe her or him, just that he needed to touch her. "A trip to England is one helluva present."

"It might have been if I was supposed to come back."

His hand stilled. Turning her so he was looking directly at her, he asked, "He was sending you away? Why?"

"A combination of things. You knew my father. He was a difficult man to please. I never did."

The short sentences told him more than a long explanation would have. She had given him the tip of the iceberg, but he wanted to see what was underneath. "What happened?"

It would have been easier to shrug off his question with a vague answer, and maybe a week ago she would have. Today she didn't.

"There was one thing my father prized almost as much as money and that was being the best at whatever he did. To be better than the best was his motto." Her mouth twisted in a crooked smile. "Especially regarding sports. He took great pride in the fact that he could play tennis and golf with the best of them and hold his own. Unfortunately I was never very good at athletics. He said I didn't have the edge when it came to competitive sports, which apparently meant I didn't want to win badly enough. He had proof of that when the Hart Corporation sponsored a swim meet on my sixteenth birthday. The press was on hand as usual. Someone was even taping it. To make a long story short, I came in dead last."

"And that was why your father was going to ship you off to your grandmother? Just because you didn't win a swim meet?"

The anger in his voice soothed her in an odd way. "It wasn't the only reason, but it was the last failure my father could accept. One disappointment too many. He never believed in the saying about it not mattering whether you win or lose. The only way he knew how to play was to win. I wasn't a winner. Plus, I embarrassed him in public, and that was the last straw. He couldn't fire me as he would one of the staff. Sending me to England was the next best thing."

The extent of Farrell Hart's cruelty shook Nick to the bone. Over the years a number of people had unburdened themselves to him, some in copious detail. None of those tales had affected him as deeply as Dionne's calm recital of her past.

He drew her back into his arms, pleased when she relaxed against him without any resistance. "You didn't use the passport."

"I didn't use the passport."

"You left Monterey."

"I left Monterey."

Pieces were falling into place, but there were

still a few missing. "Is that why you left? You didn't want to go to England?"

She sat up. "I decided if I was going to have to live with strangers in a strange place, I was going to choose where that would be. I had the money for bus fare to San Francisco, with enough left over to live on for a week at the YWCA."

"And after the first week?"

"I know more about making pizzas than I ever thought possible. I think I've washed every dish in San Francisco. Then there was the brief but busy three weeks on an assembly line putting little sprockets into big thingamajigs. I went from one job to another until I was eighteen. Then I worked as a receptionist during the day and went to school at night. When I finished high school, I needed to find a night job so I could go to school during the day."

"I'm almost afraid to ask what kind of job you found."

"I worked at a hotel reception desk on the night shift. It was an education in itself. I learned that a lot of people are up and around at all hours of the night. I could study during the quiet times, though, so it worked out. When I turned twenty-one, I contacted a lawyer who arranged for my trust fund to be transferred from England. It made the last couple years of college much easier."

There was a great deal she had left out, but Nick didn't need to hear any more right then. The rest would come in time. All he had to do was make sure there would be time. For a few minutes he simply held her, needing to feel her in his arms. There wasn't anything he could do about the past, but there was something he could do about her present. His arms tightened around her. And maybe her future.

"Dionne?"

She sighed wearily. "No more questions, Nick. The details are boring."

"Just one more." He lifted his hand to touch the side of her face, his fingers sliding into her hair. "Why are you finally telling me about your past? You didn't want to a few days ago."

"A few days ago you might have been tempted to write about me. Now I don't think you will."

"Why not?"

She smiled. "That's two questions."

"You didn't completely answer the first one. Why have you changed your mind about me? I'm still a journalist, the same as I was before."

Dionne met his gaze as she raised her hand to grasp his wrist. Slowly she slid his hand down her throat, watching his eyes darken with arousal as she brought his fingers to her breast.

Her voice was low and husky. "You didn't want me this badly before."

Unable to stop himself, he curved his fingers to mold her soft breast. She quivered under his touch, and he could see the naked longing in her eyes. Dropping his hands to her waist, he lifted her across his thighs. "I have never," he said roughly against her mouth, "wanted anyone or anything this badly before."

His mouth covered hers in a slow, deep kiss that had her fingers clenching in his shirt. He found the loose hem of her T-shirt and slid his hand under it to caress her hot silky skin. With a deft twist of his fingers he released the hook of her bra, allowing him the freedom of her body.

Dionne felt him shudder against her when he insinuated his hand between them to stroke her breast. He broke away from her mouth, and she moaned in protest, then she gasped as he buried his face between her breasts. Her hands clutched his shoulders as his lips closed around the tip of her breast through the thin cotton of her T-shirt.

Throwing her head back, she whispered his name as pleasure flooded through her. She didn't even think of resisting. She couldn't think, only feel. When he took her other breast in his mouth, she bent her head to nuzzle her face in his hair. Molten heat spread from her breasts, flowing like lava to all parts of her body. His hand covered her one breast, its hot pressure a marked contrast to the moist trailing of his tongue on the other.

When he brought his mouth back to hers, she met his passionate demand with her own. Her fingers delved into his hair to keep his lips on hers, her senses reeling with the multitude of sensations coursing through her.

Nick realized reality had ceased to exist for Dionne, so it was up to him to rein in his raging desire. Resting his head on her shoulder, he breathed in her scent as he tried to hang on to his control.

Suddenly he froze. Lifting his head, he swore under his breath as a faint sound filtered through the walls.

Bewildered by his withdrawal, Dionne spoke his name.

He smiled stiffly. "Bernice is vacuuming in the next room."

She slumped against him as his words dissipated the haze of desire.

After he refastened her bra, he gently set her aside and stood up. Clamping his fists on his hips to keep them from reaching for her, he asked, "Do you think we can get out of here for a while?"

Still dazed, she stared up at him. Without his arms around her she felt chilled and abandoned. "Where would we go?"

His eyes gleamed. "How do you feel about taking a little ride?"

Holding on to one of the shelves, she stood up. "Give me five minutes to change."

He gave her jeans and T-shirt a thorough examination, ending with the soft curves of her breasts. "You're dressed just right for where we're going. I've already told Bernie you'll be gone for the day. All you need is a jacket."

Dionne didn't argue or even ask where they were going. She didn't care. Sitting beside him as he drove away from the Hart estate, she knew wherever he was taking her, it would be someplace where they could be alone.

She wasn't surprised when he took the turnoff to Carmel Valley. His ranch was the logical place.

Even though he had left the top down on his car, the stiff breezes did little to cool the longing throbbing along her veins.

However, she was surprised when she saw his home. He turned off the road onto a smooth gravel drive, which was lined with three-row board fences on either side. Several horses grazed contentedly in the field on her right. Trees blocked her view of the house until they rounded a slight curve in the lane.

The late morning sun beat down on the white adobe walls and red tile roof of the Spanish-style house. A profusion of dark green shrubs and plants decorated the front, and a flagstone walkway led to the carved wooden door. A cypress tree with its sprawling distorted trunk and branches grew at one side of the house; geraniums bloomed alongside the shrubs, their red flowers bright against the deep green leaves.

Nick parked near one of the hitching rails and came around to open her door. Extending his hand to her, he helped her out of the car.

Dionne glanced at the hitching rail. "Nice touch."

"I didn't have the heart to take them out. Maybe I watched too many John Wayne movies when I was a kid."

She shook her head and ran her hand over the weathered wood. "No. I agree with you. They belong here." Her gaze took in all the house and pastures. "You have a lovely place, Nick."

"I'm glad you like it." He had pictured her there

since the first time he had touched her. "Would you like the grand tour?"

Desire, just under her skin, thrummed through her. "Starting with the house?"

After holding her gaze for a long moment, he held out his hand. She placed hers in it.

Nick pushed open the door and stepped aside, waiting for her to enter. She didn't. It wasn't that she had changed her mind. It was too late for that. Yet taking that irreversible step was more difficult than she had expected it to be.

Looking down at her, Nick saw the hesitation and the desire. He understood both. He had also waited as long as he could.

Lifting her up, he carried her into his house. She caught glimpses of soft beige and light blue upholstered furniture in the living room and a white pine dining table set in a small alcove.

Instead of going into his bedroom, he stopped outside the door. Very slowly he released her legs, holding her tightly in front of him. "Dionne, it would be too easy for me to carry you to my bed. If this is what you want, you need to make that choice on your own. I don't want you to tell me later you have any regrets."

She took a few steps into his room, then turned to face him. This time she held her hand out to him. "There will be no regrets, Nick."

He hesitated for a moment, awed by her beauty. The light from a window overlooking a shimmering swimming pool made her hair appear like golden-spun glass. He took her hand, then let his other hand slide along her neck and through her hair. He knew how she would taste now, but each time he kissed her, he discovered something new. It seemed as though he had waited forever for her, and now she would be his.

Dionne fell willingly into the abyss of desire that was both familiar and foreign. She had promised no regrets, and she had meant it. She wanted him to possess her, if only this once. She needed to feel his hands all over her, his hard body against hers. The memories were going to have to last a long time.

Her shirt and bra were swept away by his sure touch, his lips and hands finding intoxicating tastes and scents, new pleasures and familiar ones. An exquisite warmth filled her as his hands swept over her before he eased her down onto the bed. A button flew from his shirt as he wrenched it off, letting it fall to the floor. She clutched the smooth spread under her as his weight crushed her into the mattress.

Needs escalated. Kisses were no longer enough to quench the fires that had been smoldering between them.

When her hands smoothed over his back, he thought he would explode. He wanted to savor each moment, to linger over her silky skin and delicious feminine curves, but he was too desperate for her.

Dispensing with her jeans, he left her for a moment to tear off the remainder of his own clothing. His heated gaze locked with hers as he stood beside the bed. There was no fear or hesitation in her eyes, only a need as deep as his own.

Parting her legs, he returned to her, shuddering as his heated flesh came in contact with hers. Her eyes closed briefly, then opened to meet his searing gaze. When he felt her thighs tighten around his hips, his control snapped.

His mouth against hers, he murmured her name as he sheathed his aching flesh in her velvety warmth. She pressed her hips up to meet him, unconsciously urging him to leap with her into the sensual flames waiting for them. Hearts raced. Their breathing quickened and grew ragged.

The world splintered around them as they reached for the pinnacle of pleasure.

And found shattering satisfaction.

Eight

Nick dragged badly needed air into his lungs. It was odd. He had been breathing all of his life and now he seemed to have forgotten how.

A small rational part of his mind knew he was crushing her, but he wasn't sure he could make his body respond to the order to move. Gradually, as the fever in his blood subsided, he was able to compromise by shifting to his side, still holding her close.

Her breathing was slow and steady as she lay in his arms, her face buried in his neck. Brushing his lips over her bare shoulder, he murmured, "I love you, Dionne."

He felt her body go rigid, heard her breath catch in her throat. Easing her away enough to see her face, he read shock in her eyes. "Is it so hard to believe?"

She swallowed painfully. "You can't."

Rolling onto his back, he brought her with him, enjoying the feel of her beasts crushed against his chest. "I wouldn't have given odds against it happening either," he said, brushing damp tendrils of hair away from her face. "I gave up thinking it ever would. Not the happy-ever-after kind of love where you're incomplete unless you have someone else in your life. I really didn't believe it existed." His fingers trailed lightly down her back, and she shivered under the soft caress. "Just because I've never felt it before doesn't mean I don't know what it is. I love you."

She shook her head. "You don't have to say that, Nick. Other women might have to hear that to rationalize going to bed with a man, but I don't expect it."

If she was trying to make him angry, he thought, she wasn't succeeding. She might not believe him now, but she would—eventually.

He gently lifted her away from him and got out of the bed. As much as he would prefer to stay there with her for the rest of the day, his instincts told him to give her some space.

Instead of reaching for his clothes, he stood unabashedly naked beside the bed, looking down at her. "I'm going for a quick swim. You can join me if you like, or you can take a shower. Then I'll give you a tour of the ranch."

Without waiting for her to answer he walked out of his bedroom. A few minutes later Dionne heard the sound of a splash as he dove into the pool.

Still reeling from his declaration of love, she remained on his bed staring at the ceiling. The ramifications were frightening, yet she couldn't stop remembering the soft expression in his eyes when he had told her he loved her. If she let herself believe him, she might suffer more pain than she thought she could endure when she left Monterey.

Almost as much pain as loving him was causing her now.

She stared up at the ceiling, shock ricocheting through her. Good Lord, she thought in astonishment. It was true. She was in love with Nick.

She could argue with herself from now until doomsday and it wouldn't make any difference. What she was feeling had to be love. Even though she had never experienced anything like this overpowering need to be with Nick, to hear his voice and feel his touch, she knew it was love. There was no other explanation.

And she could do nothing to change the way she felt. Nor did she want to. With Nick, she was alive. Because of Nick, she felt complete. Without Nick, she would be more alone than she had ever been.

Nick was on his third lap when he felt the impact of someone diving into the pool. Treading water, he waited for Dionne to surface. He could see her underneath briefly before she emerged only a foot away from him. Her hair was slicked back, darker now that it was wet. Droplets of moisture glistened on her skin, making him ache to remove each drop with his tongue.

She was smiling.

"Feel like racing?" he asked, grinning.

She shook her head, her eyes glittering in the bright sunlight. Surprising them both, she placed her hands on his shoulders. It was the first time she had touched him first, and it rocked him more than the greatest intimacy with anyone else.

"No one has ever said they loved me before, Nick. That doesn't mean I'm taking what you said lightly."

"I'll just have to keep saying I love you until you believe me."

The impact of their wet, naked bodies touching created a hot whirlpool of desire deep within them.

The water was deliciously cool, the sun unrelentingly warm as it beat down on them. Nick clasped his hands at her waist and lifted her partially out of the water, exposing her breasts. Water cascaded over her, and he licked away the droplets beading on her taut nipples. Her fingers dug into his shoulders as she threw her head back. With her eyes closed she felt the sun on her face as his mouth closed around her breast.

The water ebbed around her as he slowly lowered her back into the pool, her body sliding against his, tormenting and tantalizing them both. Her legs clasped his hips as he kissed her hungrily.

His tongue surged into her mouth at the same time as he slid into her body.

• • •

Dionne picked a piece of straw off the front of her T-shirt and leaned on the handle of a pitchfork. "You sure know how to show a girl a great time, Lyon," she said lightly. "Mucking out horse stalls is definitely the highlight of the tour."

Grinning, Nick emptied the load on his pitchfork into the wheelbarrow. "I'm not the one who's led a sheltered life. You asked what it was used for. Now you know."

Walking alongside him as he wheeled the barrow out of the barn, she said, "I didn't realize you were only trying to improve my mind when you put me to work cleaning out the stalls." Outside, she looked around. "I'm going to hate to leave."

He tipped the contents of the wheelbarrow onto the compost heap behind the barn. "Then don't." After brushing his hands off on his thighs, he left the wheelbarrow where it was and took her arm. "Come on," he said, starting toward the house. "I'll feed you. It's the least I can do after all that pitchforking."

"When you first told me you lived on a ranch, I was surprised. Somewhere out in the country, away from city lights and activity didn't fit the image I had of you."

"It was an old image. I'm no longer an eighteen-year-old hotshot who thinks he knows all the answers."

No, he wasn't, she reflected. He was much more.

"It's funny," she mused aloud. "I thought I had all the answers until I came back to Monterey. All those years, I lived under the misconception that I was on my own, that my father had decided to write me off. I wasn't so naive I didn't think he could find me if he tried. When a year passed and I didn't hear from him, I concluded he couldn't care less what I did. I was so proud of myself for making a life of my own without help from him or anyone else. Now I'm ruining other people's lives, people like the Canaveris."

"Dionne, you aren't responsible for their lives. They are."

They were approaching the house, and Dionne stopped to lean against the hitching rail. "There's something I don't understand. My father was supposed to be such a financial wizard. I certainly couldn't find any sign of that in the records, at least not for the last couple of years. He made bad investments, like buying that schoolhouse from the city when it was condemned. Property taxes weren't paid on some of the property, and the major share of the corporation's assets are gone. It doesn't make sense. The corporation was all he ever thought of, all he ever cared about. You knew him, Nick, probably better than I did. Why would he let it all go down the drain?"

"Maybe he found something he thought was more important than money."

She crossed her arms over her chest. "What could Farrell Hart possibly find more important than money?"

"Love."

Her mouth dropped open in amazement. "You've

got to be joking. He never knew the meaning of the word."

Nick touched her cheek. "I didn't either, Dionne."

She wanted to argue with him, considering who he was talking about, but she had learned how powerful love was with Nick. Perhaps her father had discovered deeper feelings for someone other than himself. Anything was possible, she supposed. It gave her something to think about regarding Leah Buckner and her son. Having met his last mistress, though, Dionne had trouble believing her father had found more with Leah Buckner than the temporary relationship he'd had with all the others.

Nick tipped her chin up so she would look at him. "I brought you out here to get you away from the problems at the estate. They will still be there when you go back, so forget about them for now."

It was what she wanted too. She didn't want her time with Nick marred by thoughts of her father and the debts waiting to be paid. All she wanted was to immerse herself in the pleasure of his company.

"I'm in your hands," she said, smiling slowly.

"Exactly where you should be," he said seriously.

And that was where she stayed for the rest of the day. Whether they were walking around the ranch, feeding the horses, or fixing something to eat, Nick was always touching her. A casual arm over her shoulders, holding her hand, brushing against her, sitting beside her.

The sensual attraction didn't diminish as the

day progressed, nor was their lovemaking con-
fined to the bedroom. A brief kiss in the barn led
to an erotic adventure on clean, fresh-smelling
hay. A second cooling swim generated a second
passionate encounter in the pool. By evening
Dionne felt every particle of her being saturated
with Nick's intense attention.

But it had to end.

They were sitting out by the pool when she told
Nick she really should be leaving.

Sprawled out on the chaise longue with a towel
draped around his hips, he murmured, "Why?"

The lights around the pool were the only illumi-
nation, enough for Dionne to see he had his eyes
closed. She felt a warm glow of happiness just
looking at him. It had been a wonderful day, one
she would remember forever, a memory to bring
out some lonely night when she was back in her
apartment.

Wearing only her T-shirt and panties, she un-
coiled her legs and reached for her jeans, which
were lying across the end of her lounge chair. "It's
getting late. I have to go back to the estate."

Opening his eyes, he watched her tug on her
jeans. It was going to be a waste of time, he
mused, since he would just have to take them off
her again.

"I didn't realize you had a curfew."

"No. It's, well, I, you see . . ."

Chuckling, he suddenly sat up, grabbed her
hand, and pulled her over onto his lap. "Clear as a
bell. I understand perfectly."

His hand slid under her shirt to cover her breast as he kissed her. "There is no reason for you to go back to the estate, and a number of reasons to stay here with me. Call Bernie and tell her you won't be back tonight."

"Are you asking me to stay?"

"No," he said against her throat. "I'm telling you."

Dionne felt his fingers at the snap of her jeans, then the zipper was lowered. His hand slid across her stomach, and lower.

She wrapped her arms around his neck and fell head first into the world of sensuality Nick had introduced her to.

Dionne was taking a fresh shirt of Nick's off the hanger in the walk-in closet when her bare toes banged into a hard, cold object. Slipping the shirt on, she glanced down, then bent over to get a closer look. How strange, she thought, picking it up. It was heavier than she expected. She turned to Nick, who was pulling on his jeans.

"Why do you have an antique fire engine in your closet?"

He came over to her and looked down at the toy. "So that's where it was. Camilla's boy must have left it there."

"Who's Camilla?"

"She comes once a week to clean. Sometimes she brings her son with her, and he plays with my antique toys. He's supposed to put them back when he's through, but as you can see, that doesn't always happen."

"You collect antique toys?"

"It didn't start out that way. My grandmother wanted to make sure I wouldn't break any of the toys she gave me, so they were all made of cast iron. I received one every Christmas and birthday until she died seven years ago."

"She continued to send them even after you grew up?" Dionne asked, amused.

He grinned. "Sure. I would have been disappointed if she hadn't." Tucking the fire engine under his arm, he took her hand. "Come on. I'll show them to you."

He kept the toys in the den, and all of them were in their original boxes. She sat on the floor as he pulled the boxes out of a cupboard to one side of the fireplace. He obviously wouldn't be satisfied until she'd seen every single one. There were tractors, trucks, cars, stagecoaches, and a few mechanical toy banks. She found it oddly touching he had kept the toys. He wasn't a bit self-conscious about admitting he had saved them and still treasured them.

While she was putting a penny in a miniature bulldog's gaping mouth, he said, "Fair is fair. Now you know about my secret hoard of toys. What did you collect as a child?"

She watched the bulldog hop through a hoop and deposit the penny in the slot on top of a fireplug, then answered him. "After she left, my mother sent me a music box on my birthday. My

favorite had a man and a woman dressed in pe-
riod clothing from the court of St. James. They
waltzed around and around to 'The Blue Danube.'
It was the only thing I took with me when I left,
other than a few items of clothing."

"Do you still have it?"

She nodded, setting the bank down onto the
floor. "It's on the dresser in my bedroom at the
estate. I brought it back with me."

Pleased she was finding it easier to let him into
her past, he swept the toys to one side and eased
her down onto the rug. "We'll introduce your posh
dancers to my sturdy toys," he murmured against
her mouth. "Later."

That evening Nick turned on the outside lights
so they could see their way to the barn after the
sun went down. They made sure the horses were
all in and comfortable for the night, then walked
leisurely back to the house, at ease with the day
and each other. The air was clear with a slight
breeze. The only sound was the crunch of their
footsteps on the lightly graveled path between the
barn and the house. Occasionally the breeze would
rustle the leaves of the cypress trees.

Nick tightened his arm around her waist, and
she looked up. "What are you thinking about?" she
asked.

"So far you've cleaned out their stalls, helped
feed them, and you obviously like them, but I've
never asked if you ride horses."

"I learned to ride English-style, my parents' idea of the way proper little ladies should ride. I switched to a Western saddle at a summer camp for disadvantaged kids when I worked there a few years ago. They wouldn't be caught dead on one of those sissy saddles, as they called them."

"You like working with children, don't you? Especially kids with problems."

She shrugged, making light of a subject she felt very serious about. "All kids have problems. It's not easy being a child. One with learning disabilities has an even harder time. I get a great deal of satisfaction out of helping a child learn to read and write."

Nick stopped and hugged her. "You'll have to tell them that when they grow up, they'll be able to read 'The Lyon's Roar' column written by that immensely talented Nicholas Lyon."

Slipping her arms around him, she smiled. "I'll make it required reading."

If Dionne had written the scenario for the perfect weekend, she wouldn't have been able to come up with anything better than the one she spent with Nick. Everything else receded into the background; her financial problems, Leah Buckner and her son, and San Francisco.

However, reality intruded rudely on Sunday afternoon when Bernie phoned the ranch, asking to speak to Dionne. In a few short sentences she managed to burst the bubble of happiness Dionne had been living in.

Hanging up the phone, Dionne turned to Nick. "Something's come up. I have to go back to the estate."

He studied her carefully. The defeated slump of her shoulders and the strained look in her eyes had returned. Whatever Bernie had told her, it hadn't been good news. And she wasn't telling him what it was. He had hoped they had gotten to the point where she now trusted him. Apparently they hadn't.

This time he didn't ask why or try to talk her out of it. He simply stepped aside so she could pass him, then followed her out to his car.

Dionne was silent during the drive. Coming back to reality so suddenly had numbed her, as though she had been plunged into ice-cold water.

When Nick drove up to the front of the house, he parked behind a late model Mercedes. "It looks like you have company."

"It looks that way." Her expression was closed.

He started to shut off the engine, but she reached over to stop him. "I don't want you to come in with me, Nick. This is something I have to take care of by myself."

"Who is it?"

Instead of answering him, she opened the door. He grabbed her arm before she could get out of the car. "You're shutting me out, Dionne," he said tightly. "Why? I thought we'd gotten past that this weekend."

She shook her head. "This has nothing to do with this weekend, Nick."

"It has something to do with you, and whatever it is, it's upsetting you."

"It's something I have to take care of on my own. I would just as soon not involve you, Nick."

"If you're involved, so am I."

"Not with this."

She wrenched her arm out of his hold and left the car.

Nick didn't attempt to follow her, only watching as she ran up the front steps and disappeared into the house. His fingers tightened on the wheel to keep him from going after her. Or strangling her.

He had been a fool, he thought angrily, a lovesick fool, wallowing in the joy of loving Dionne. He had thought all the hurdles had been overcome when she had given herself to him. Maybe some men could accept possessing a woman's body without regard to her thoughts and feelings. He wasn't one of them. Nor was he a man to be put off by a setback. His eyes narrowed with determination. He would give her a little space, then close in.

Dionne didn't move from the door until she heard Nick drive away. Then she walked toward the living room. She didn't bother changing clothes before she confronted her father's mistress. The other woman probably wouldn't notice, nor would Dionne care if she did.

Leah Buckner was pacing the floor, a drink in her hand. Her emerald-green leather dress was skin tight with a slit part way up one slender thigh. Time and acquaintance hadn't improved Dionne's opinion of the woman, who put her makeup on with a trowel.

Dionne stepped into the room. "What's so urgent that it can't wait until tomorrow, Miss Buckner?"

Whirling around, Leah spilled some of her drink onto her dress and the floor. It was typical of her, at least from what Dionne had seen of the other woman. Leah was sometimes impulsive, sometimes irrational, and all the time a royal pain in the tush. She was also strikingly beautiful with raven hair and classic features that wouldn't be out of place on the cover of a fashion magazine.

Leah plunked her wet glass down on an antique end table and faced Dionne with her hands on her hips. "I'm tired of waiting, Miss Hart." She held up a manicured hand as Dionne started to speak. "I know. I'm supposed to wait until the lawyers work things out. I talk to mine. You talk to yours. They talk to each other. It's all a waste of time."

Dionne sat down on the couch, casually crossing one leg over the other. Her experiences as a teacher of difficult, recalcitrant children helped her in dealing with the excitable woman. The more emotional Leah acted, the calmer Dionne became.

"I told you before, Miss Buckner. There isn't anything I can do until the problems with the estate are settled."

"Then settle them. I've done everything I was told to do. I put Sammy through those awful tests at the hospital. I haven't gone to the newspapers." She began pacing again. "All I've been doing is waiting, waiting, waiting."

"If I could change things, I would," Dionne said. "Believe me, there isn't anything I would like better than to have someone wave a magic wand to make the mess my father left disappear."

Stopping, Leah turned abruptly. "You wish I would disappear. And my son. That way you can keep all the money for yourself."

Striving for patience, Dionne said quietly, "I'm not enjoying this delay any more than you are. There is only so much I can do. It's mostly in the lawyers' hands now."

Tears glistened in the other woman's eyes, and she dabbed at them delicately with the tips of her fingers. "If Farrell were alive, he would do something about this."

"If Farrell were alive, we wouldn't need to be having this conversation," Dionne murmured.

"I find it hard to believe you're Farrell's daughter," Leah said with an almost convincing sob. "He would have found some way around all this legal garbage. He always took very good care of me and Sammy. I know he would want you to do everything you can so we will be provided for now that he's gone."

Weary of going over the same thing again, Dionne stood up. "I realize you don't believe me, Miss Buckner, but if the tests prove your son is my father's and if there is any money left, I'll see that you both benefit. That's the best I can do."

"Well, it isn't good enough. I need money now."

Here it comes, Dionne thought. Each conversation ended with the same thing, a demand for money. Next would be a threat.

"I'm sure," Leah went on, "the local newspapers would be happy to run a story on how Farrell Hart's daughter is mistreating her two-year-old half brother."

Nodding, Dionne agreed. "I'm sure they would be." She sighed. "How much do you need to tide you over until this thing is settled " Or until the next time you need money, Dionne added silently.

Leah's tears faded away as though by magic. She quoted an exorbitant amount, as usual, which Dionne had no intention of paying even if she could. Leaving Leah for a few minutes, she returned with some cash in an envelope.

"This will have to do, Miss Buckner. It won't buy caviar, but it will be enough for you to purchase food for you and your son."

Leah stuffed the envelope in a small clutch purse she had left on one of the tables. Her spiked heels were loud on the bare floor in the foyer as she left without so much as a thank-you.

Dionne returned to the couch and sat down, leaning her head back and closing her eyes. She hated the feeling of being used and manipulated, but as before in previous meetings with her father's mistress, she took the only way out to end each confrontation. She gave the woman money.

It wasn't just to get rid of her. Leah Buckner had been involved with Farrell Hart for four years. He had provided well for her while he was alive and apparently had cared for the woman. At least as much as he was capable of caring for anyone, Dionne supposed. He had been Leah's only means of support. Now that he was gone, Dionne felt obligated to do something until the final reckoning of the estate could be made.

Leah's threat to go running to a reporter had something to do with it too. It was bad enough to be responsible for the situation her father had left behind. To have the whole peninsula aware of Farrell Hart's financial disasters was a legacy she didn't want. It was odd that she felt a peculiar loyalty to the man she hadn't seen in fourteen years, wanting to be discreet about his affairs, both financial and personal.

Her thoughts drifted to Nick. His anger had been justified when she left his car so abruptly without any explanation. Especially after the weekend they had spent together.

If she couldn't explain her actions to herself, though, how could she explain them to him?

A tree branch almost beheaded Nick as he rode the horse too fast in the dark. He had done sev-

eral foolish things in his day, but he was topping
them all tonight.

Pulling on the reins, he slowed the horse's pace.
If he wasn't careful, he could break either his
neck or the horse's while he was trying to run off
his anger. Swimming laps in the pool hadn't
helped. Pacing up and down in his house hadn't
accomplished a thing either. And all he'd managed to do in the last half hour was get the horse
as lathered as he was.

When he returned to his house, he saw a familiar car parked in front. It looked like every light
had been turned on inside, as well as all the outside ones. As usual, Marty had made himself at
home.

Nick took time to cool down his horse before he
went into the house. Marty was slouched down in
a chair with his feet propped up on the coffee
table. He was holding a can of beer in his hand.
Four inches shorter than Nick, Martin Lawson
had a deceptively cherubic face. A lawyer, he was
known as a tough nut in the courtroom.

Nick crossed the room and plopped down on
the couch, stretching out on his back. "What'd
Sally do now?"

Marty grunted. "She wants me to meet her
mother."

A corner of Nick's mouth twitched. Marty made
it sound as though his girlfriend was threatening
him with the guillotine. "Sounds serious."

"You're telling me," Marty grumbled, finishing
off the beer. "This was your last beer."

"You are having a bad day, aren't you?"

His friend gave him a long, probing look. "You aren't exactly turning cartwheels either, pal. Having a little spell of writer's block?"

Frowning, Nick placed his hands under his head and stared up at the ceiling. "No."

"You just decided to go riding in the middle of the night for the heck of it?"

"No."

"You would be a real joy on the witness stand. Just full of juicy details. Do you think you could be a bit more specific? Like who the woman is?"

The frown turned into a scowl. "Why does it have to be a woman?"

"What else could it be?" Marty dropped his feet onto the floor and sat forward. "I don't believe it. Some woman has finally put Nicholas Lyon on the rack." He slapped his hand on his thigh. "This is great. I thought I'd never see the day. Who is she?"

"Dionne Hart."

Nick had heard of someone's jaw dropping, but he had never seen it happen—until now. At any other time he might have thought it was funny. Marty certainly did. His friend's laughter filled the room.

"I'm glad you're enjoying this, Marty."

Holding his side, Marty grinned. "I am enjoying it, Nick. So what's the problem, other than the fact that her father was one of the biggest—"

"It's complicated." In one sudden move Nick got to his feet. "I think there's more beer in the small refrigerator behind the bar," he said as he started in that direction. "You want another one?"

"I already looked. There isn't any. Don't change the subject."

Grabbing a soft drink, Nick returned to the couch and sat down. "I thought you came here to talk about your problems with Sally."

"I did. She wants me to meet her mother. I'm not about to put my foot into that trap. End of my problem. What's yours?"

Nick smiled crookedly. "I don't know, Marty. That's the problem."

Nine

Because he had been giving all his time to Dionne, Nick had been neglecting his work. But that wasn't the only reason he didn't call or go see her for three days.

He needed time to regroup. Just when he had thought they were the closest two people could ever be, she had left him in the driveway with no explanation other than her problems were her business and not his.

She couldn't have made that clearer if she had proclaimed it in neon letters. Soon she was going to learn that what affected her was his business too.

He flicked on his computer and stared at the screen, his mind on Dionne rather than the column he needed to write. All he had to do was figure out how he was going to convince Dionne he was in for the long haul, for better or worse, thick or thin, in sickness and in health. Realizing the direction he was going, he forced his attention back to the screen.

By Wednesday Dionne's frustration—at the hassle of settling her father's estate and at her self-imposed estrangement from Nick—was at an all-time high. After Leah Buckner had left Sunday evening, Dionne had been tempted to call Nick. But realizing she couldn't explain her abrupt departure, she had stayed away from the phone. When she arrived at the Hart Corporation offices Monday morning, she decided not to call him until she'd finished working through the mess her father had left her. Her preoccupation with it was simply a barrier between her and Nick, and she wanted it out of the way before she saw him again. Of course, if he showed up on her doorstep, she wouldn't turn him away.

To her disappointment he didn't come to see her. He didn't even call. She turned aside her hurt, concentrating on the final sales and deals the lawyers and realtors had arranged, signing papers and accepting an offer for her father's house.

By Wednesday afternoon she was reaching for her last ounce of patience to finalize everything so she could go to Nick. After she finished at the office, she had to supervise the packing of furniture at the estate. She chafed at the delays, even though they couldn't be avoided. It seemed like months instead of only days since she had seen Nick.

Except for doing his chores around the ranch, he stayed at his desk all of Wednesday. Usually when he was working, his concentration was total, his mind only on the article he was writing. That was before Dionne. Now she was part of his life, part of him. It was odd how content he'd thought he had been in the past. Since meeting Dionne, he felt complete only when he was with her. There was no other way to describe how she made him feel.

She was also driving him crazy. He was a man who liked to know where he stood. No, he corrected himself. He was a man who *had* to know where he stood, and with Dionne he hadn't the faintest idea. During the weekend he'd thought he knew. Now he didn't.

Only when they made love did he feel completely sure of her. She responded fully, giving herself over to the fiery passion engendered between them. But they couldn't live their whole lives in bed. Their lovemaking was exciting and wonderful, yet he wanted more.

The phone rang, cutting in on his thoughts. After the third ring, he picked it up. Without bothering with the pleasantries, Barry Kregor got right to the point. "You let me down, boy. I was counting on you to give me any story concerning

Dionne Hart. I have to hear about it from my barber."

Holding the phone in the crook of his neck, Nick leaned back in his chair and propped his feet on his desk. "Hear what?"

"That the Hart Corporation has donated a building to be used as a sports training center. Free and clear. As is. Any renovations have to be done by volunteers or supporters. It's still a terrific thing for the kids."

Nick's feet came crashing down to the floor as he sat up. "What are you talking about? What building?"

Barry gave him an address and the area where the building was located.

"When did this all happen?" Nick asked.

"I heard about it an hour ago when I got a haircut. All Fred knows is that one of his other patrons mentioned it this morning. This guy is the president of that amateur sports club you belong to, but do you tell your good friend Barry about this? Oh, no. Obviously you don't think giving a building away is news, especially when Farrell Hart's daughter is doing the donating."

"I didn't know anything about it, Barry."

"Well, now you do, so go get me the story. I'd like a photograph of Miss Hart in front of the building. Find out if there's going to be a ribbon cutting, or when the papers will be signed, or if they already have. Whatever you can get is more than I got now. I'd send one of my reporters, but Miss Hart won't talk to anyone. You know her.

You get the story. And you'd better hurry. Thornton came back and said there's a moving van parked in front of the Hart estate."

If Barry had more to say, Nick didn't hear it. He had hung up the phone and was across the room in two seconds. In less than a minute he was behind the wheel of his car. He hadn't taken the time to turn off his computer or any of the lights. He didn't give them a thought.

There was no moving van in front of the estate when he pulled up. There were also no lights visible from the outside. Taking two steps at a time, he ran up to the front door. It was locked. He hurried around to the side of the house and saw Dionne's car parked near the back entrance. He tried that door, but it was also locked.

He knew of only one other door. As he raced around the corner of the house he saw a thread of light where the curtains came together over the French doors. As he approached them he heard music.

Putting his hand on the door latch, he turned it, grunting in satisfaction when it clicked open. He parted the curtains and stepped into the living room.

All of the elegant furnishings were gone. The room had been stripped of everything, except for a trunk, the old wooden table from the kitchen, a bedroll, and several candles burning in the middle of the table. Also on the table was a cassette player, which was where the music was coming from. The song was a rousing rendition of "The

Charleston" rag. It sounded tinny, as though it were a copy of an old record from the Roaring Twenties.

Dionne was sitting on the floor using the bedroll as a backrest. In one hand was a stemmed glass, and he saw a bottle of champagne near her on the floor.

Whether because of the movement of the curtain or the cool air, she looked up. When she saw him, she lifted the glass as though making a toast.

He saw her lips move, but couldn't hear what she said over the loud music. Crossing the room, he punched the stop button on the cassette player.

"Would you like some champagne?" she asked, still holding the glass up.

The bubbles danced and popped in the glass, but he didn't take it. "Good Lord, Dionne, you're sloshed. What's the occasion?"

She shrugged and took a sip of champagne. "This is the only bottle I kept out of my father's wine cellar before I sold it. It seems appropriate somehow to drink a bottle of his finest champagne on the day the movers emptied his house."

Nick picked up the bottle. "The house isn't the only thing that's almost empty."

She giggled. "It's good champagne. My father bought nothing but the best."

"And you sold it all," he murmured as he set the bottle down on the table, out of her reach.

She shook her head. "Not all of it was sold. The lawyer and the banks have made arrangements with some of the people who had been leasing various properties. You'll be pleased to hear the Canaveris were allowed to apply all of the rent they've paid over the years to the purchase price. The balance will be financed with payments they can manage. Some of the ways the lawyer and his staff worked things out were a little complicated, but everything has been sold, turned over, or written off for taxes."

"Or given away like the building you gave to the Special Olympics."

"That too."

"You've been busy."

She frowned. It didn't sound like a compliment. In fact, Nick appeared to be downright peeved about something. "The lawyer has been busy. All I've done is sign documents."

Nick hitched up his jeans and knelt in front of her so he could see her face. "So now what?"

She blinked, then looked at him with a glazed blue stare. "Now what, what?" she muttered, feeling as stupid as her question sounded.

Exasperation tightened his mouth, and he stood up, taking several steps away from her. "You're in no condition to drive."

He wasn't making any sense. Or perhaps it was her. She hadn't had as much champagne as he thought she had. Bernie had had a glass before she left, and the movers had gladly gulped down a glass each. Still, the two glasses she had drunk must have gone straight to her head, because she was having great difficulty understanding him.

"Since I'm not going anywhere, it doesn't really matter, does it?" she asked.

"You were just going to leave, weren't you? Without even a phone call."

The doorbell rang, but Dionne made no move to answer it. It rang again, this time longer and more insistent. Whoever it was, Nick realized he or she didn't plan on going away without a little persuasion. He was in the right mood to discourage anyone from interfering. When he opened the door, he half-expected to see a reporter. He certainly wasn't expecting an irate woman who barged right past him. Dressed all in black from her silk blouse to skintight pants and heels, she pulled a small boy along with her. In the other hand she clutched several papers.

"Where's Dionne Hart?" she demanded, but didn't give him a chance to answer. "Never mind. I'll find her myself."

Tugging the little boy along with her, she marched toward the living room. Nick was right on her heels. The moment she spotted Dionne, she started waving the papers in the air.

"How dare you pawn this pittance settlement off on me! This is an insult."

Dionne didn't bother getting up. "It's the best we could do, Miss Buckner."

"Well, it's not good enough." She thrust the boy in front of her. "Sammy is your father's child. The tests prove it. If you think I'm going to agree to this ridiculous arrangement, you're very much mistaken."

Dionne set her glass down on the floor. "Miss Buckner," she said patiently, "I've told you more times than I care to count that my father left only debts, no capital of any kind. The arrangement the lawyer was able to make will give you the income from two of the properties we were able to save. It's not the lump sum you wanted, but they are long-term leases and will provide you and your son with a comfortable income. I'm sorry, but it's the best we could manage."

Whether it was from being dragged around, the loud voices, or the strange surroundings, the little boy began to cry. Nick stared from the child to the irate woman, then to Dionne. "Dionne, what's going on?" he asked.

The woman whirled around. "Who are you?"

"I'm Nicholas Lyon. Who are you?" he asked with equal belligerence.

Dionne answered. "This charming woman is Leah Buckner, Nick. She was . . . a friend of my father's." When Leah made no move to comfort her son, Dionne gently eased the little boy onto her lap. "And, as you can see, a devoted mother."

Leah evidently didn't care for the way she had been introduced. "I was Farrell Hart's fiancée and the mother of his child. Miss Hart doesn't want to recognize my relationship to her father, so just to keep me quiet, she makes a paltry settlement." Suddenly she stopped to stare at Nick. "Nicholas Lyon. Why is that name familiar?" Her eyes narrowed with suspicion. "Are you one of her lawyers? I thought I'd met them all."

Dionne again provided the explanation. "Nick writes a column for the newspapers, Leah. You might have read it. 'The Lyon's Roar.' You've been wanting to talk to a journalist. Here's your chance."

Nick stared at Dionne. What in hell was she up to, he wondered, completely mystified. But she hadn't finished.

"If you don't mind, I'd just as soon not listen to the interview. I've heard it all before, and I'm sure Sammy would rather not hear it either." Holding the boy in her arms, she picked up a candle. "We'll be in the kitchen."

Leah didn't even wait until Dionne had completely left the room before she began her tirade of injustices at the hands of Farrell's daughter. Dionne could hear her listing her many grievances all the way to the kitchen. Shutting the door in the hope of a bit of peace and quiet, she took a cracker out of the box Bernie had set aside with a few other tidbits.

While Sammy sat on the counter happily munching away, she examined him more closely. That morning her father's lawyer had informed her that the paternity test had come back positive. This small child was her half brother. Inspecting his facial features, she couldn't see anything of herself or her father, except perhaps for the color of his eyes. She wiped a single tear off his cheek, left over from his earlier distress.

She found herself disliking the thought of this innocent child living with Leah Buckner. Other than provide financially for his upkeep, though, there was little Dionne could do to help Sammy. She could only hope he would somehow grow up with better values than he was bound to learn from Leah Buckner.

By the time the crazy woman had finished venting her wrath, Nick had a colossal headache. Even though he was furious, his anger wasn't directed toward the whining woman. During the long tirade, he had learned Leah was the reason he had been brushed off on Sunday night. Dionne hadn't wanted him to meet Leah then, but now she did.

Dionne was using him. Leah Buckner wanted publicity, so Dionne had provided the means. Him. She had to know he wouldn't print a single word the woman said. For one thing, most of what the Buckner woman was saying was sour grapes. For another, it wasn't the type of journalism he practiced. Dionne had to realize that, even though they hadn't known each other very long.

He was barely civil as he escorted Leah to the kitchen to retrieve her son. She didn't say a word to Dionne as she gathered up the tired little boy. She apparently had nothing further to say, although Nick found that hard to believe.

To make sure the wretched woman was definitely leaving, he walked her and the boy out to her car. When he returned to the house, Dionne had carried her candle back to the bare living room and was unrolling the sleeping bag.

Before she had finished, he crossed the room and stopped her. Seizing her arms, he came just short of shaking her. "You aren't sleeping on the damn floor, and you aren't taking off for San Francisco in the morning. You've been having your own way long enough. Now it's my turn."

He extinguished the candles, then, without waiting for her to object, clamped his arm around her waist and propelled her out of the house and into his car. He buckled her seat belt for her, then his own. The drive was made in record time. Nick didn't say a word, and his expression didn't encourage Dionne to speak. It wasn't that Nick didn't have anything to say. He simply wanted both hands free when they talked, just in case he gave in to the temptation to wring her neck.

Once at his house, he marched her into the kitchen and pressed her down into a chair before making coffee. After plugging in the coffee maker, he crossed his arms over his chest and stared at her.

"What was your plan, Dionne? To send me a postcard when you were back in San Francisco? What were you going to write? It was nice knowing you? Having a wonderful time, wish you were here?"

The champagne and exhaustion were catching up with her, making it difficult for her to think clearly. Rubbing her forehead, she murmured, "During the last couple of days all I've been doing is trying to keep up with things as they happened. I haven't thought any further ahead than that."

"Well, you're going to have to try. Why don't you

start with why you left me alone with your father's girlfriend?"

She relaxed for the first time in days. "I'm sorry
about that. It wasn't fair of me to pawn her off on
you like that. I've just heard it all many times
before, and I wasn't in the mood to hear it again."

He poured coffee into two earthenware mugs
and carried them over to the table. "Why let me
meet her tonight? You didn't want me to see her
on Sunday night."

Her head jerked up. "Leah covered a great deal
during her little chat, apparently."

Nick wasn't going to be diverted. "Why, Dionne?
Why tonight and not Sunday night?"

"I wasn't ready for you to know about my father's mistress on Sunday night."

"What's changed between now and Sunday?"

"Everything came together the last couple of
days. I was finally able to settle my father's affairs.
Maybe not exactly the way I wanted to, but at
least it's over. Nothing Leah Buckner can say will
affect the proceedings now."

At last he understood. "I had it backwards, didn't
I? You didn't want your father's mistress to meet
me, not the other way around. If I met Leah Buckner on Sunday night, she would have done what
she did tonight, spilled everything to a journalist." He walked over to her and grabbed her arms,
pulling her out of the chair. "You actually thought
I would be tempted to write about her and your
father, didn't you? That would have endangered
your financial negotiations. Dammit, Dionne. I

don't write about that type of thing, and you should know that."

His fingers were digging into her arms, but she smiled. If she had slapped him, he couldn't have looked more shocked.

"Why in hell are you smiling?"

"Nick, why did you think I left you with Leah? I knew she would tell you the whole charming story, and I knew you wouldn't write it. By hearing all the juicy details for yourself you would understand more than if I had tried to explain Leah Buckner to you."

He loosened his grip and walked around the table. Slowly he sat down. "You confuse the hell out of me, lady."

Dionne came over to him and knelt in front of him. With her hands on his knees, she gazed up at him.

"Nick, it seems all I've done when we're together is moan and groan about my problems. I didn't want them to ruin the weekend. Maybe in some odd way I was trying to keep the sordid details from you because I'm not very proud of the way my father lived his life."

"I knew what kind of man your father was, Dionne. That has nothing to do with how I feel about you."

"I'm used to dealing with problems myself, without depending on anyone else. It was up to me to try to resolve the mess my father had left the best way I could. I don't have his penchant for publicity. The last thing I want is for Leah's story to be splashed all over the newspaper. She doesn't care one way or the other. In fact, I imagine she would even enjoy having the whole world know about her and my father."

"You don't owe your father anything, Dionne."

"Maybe not, but I owed the innocent people that were going to suffer financially because of him. Also I—" She broke off. "Never mind."

She started to stand up, but he clamped his hands down over hers, making her stay where she was. "Finish it."

She bit her lip for a few seconds. "It doesn't make much sense, but I felt I also owed my father to do what I could to keep his relationship with Leah Buckner quiet. You've met her. She's more concerned about money than anything else. It hasn't been easy keeping her quiet."

"Dionne, Leah Buckner isn't the first woman your father was involved with. He was never discreet about his affairs. If anything, he flaunted them." His fingers closed around hers. Pulling her between his legs, he cupped her face, tilting it up so he could look at her. "Tell me the rest."

She frowned. "That's it. Except to say I'm sorry for handling things so badly."

He shook his head. "There's more. Like what you're going to do now. You can't live in that empty house until the new owners take over. When are you going back to San Francisco?"

The frown disappeared to be replaced by a soft smile. "I guess that depends on you."

He slipped his fingers into her hair. "If it depends on me, you won't be going back to San Francisco. I love you, Dionne. I want you to stay here."

She brought her hands up to cover his. "Okay."

He could only look into her eyes for a long moment, stunned by the meaning behind that one word. "Does that mean you'll stay in Monterey?"

"No."

Confusion, bewilderment, and a trace of anger flickered through him. "Then what do you mean?"

"I'm staying in Carmel, not Monterey. Because you are here. Because you said you loved me." She paused for a moment. "And because I'm in love with you."

He wanted to believe her. More than anything in this world, he wanted to believe her. It wasn't that easy, though. Just because she said the words didn't mean she meant them in the same way he did.

Of all the questions spinning through his mind, he managed to utter only one word. "When?"

It wasn't the response Dionne had expected, and she hesitated before answering. "At fifteen I was infatuated with you. When I saw you stroll into the office that first day, I was attracted to you. Each time I've been with you since then, I've felt something growing and expanding deep inside me. I finally recognized what it was the first time we made love." Her eyes were serious and intent. "I love you, Nick. I could go back to San Francisco, but I would be leaving my heart here."

"Dionne," he groaned, lifting her at the same

time as he lowered her head. His kiss was a mixture of desperation, joy, and hunger.

Suddenly he broke away to lift her into his arms. He got up and carried her out of the kitchen, down the hall, and into his bedroom.

Easing her down on the bed, he said, "Say it again."

Dionne looked up at him, seeing the trace of uncertainty in his eyes. He still didn't fully believe her, and she couldn't blame him. She had given him a merry chase. Now it was time to cross the finish line.

Raising her hands in invitation, she murmured, "I love you, Nick."

Placing his knee on the mattress, he slowly came down on the bed with her.

Ten

They slept late the next morning and didn't leave
the ranch house the entire day except for feeding
the horses. No one else existed. They lived for
each moment, concentrating on each other. The
future was no farther than the next minute. The
only plans discussed were what to eat.

In the evening Dionne sat curled up in a comfortable chair in Nick's study, reading a book while
he worked on his column. Since she had no other
clothes with her except the ones she'd had on
when he brought her there, she was wearing one
of his shirts.

Until he turned off the computer.

She went into his arms willingly, happier than
she had ever been in her life. If she was living in a
fool's paradise, she didn't mind. Not when she
could be in Nick's arms.

The outside world intruded all too soon. Practical matters had to be faced. Dionne couldn't go around wearing his shirts forever. Nor could they continue to exist on love alone. Mundane matters such as food and clothing had to be considered, even in paradise.

While they were eating breakfast the next morning, Dionne brought up the matter of needing to get her personal belongings out of the house.

Nick turned a page of the morning paper. "We can go to the estate after—"

When he stopped abruptly, she looked up. He was staring at something in the paper, a frown creasing his brow. "What is it?"

Rather than read it to her, he folded the paper and handed it to her, tapping a column.

Puzzled, she began to read. It only took the first sentence for her heart to sink. Leah Buckner had found a reporter who was more than willing to tell her story in prurient detail. Dionne's name was mentioned several times, the facts distorted, the quotes from Leah Buckner bitter.

When she was finished, Dionne tossed the paper onto the floor. "I come off looking like a cross between Joan Crawford and the Wicked Witch of the West."

"That's only her side of it."

"It's also the only side people are going to know."

"Not if you do something about it."

For a moment Dionne simply stared at him, then comprehension widened her eyes. "You're not serious, Nick. You know how I feel about publicity."

He reached across the table and covered her hand with his. "Dionne, when a reporter smells a story, he'll dig and dig until he gets one. If you give him a bone to gnaw on, he won't go for your throat. Unless you tell your side of the situation, you can't blame people for thinking what Leah Buckner is saying is true."

"Or I can just let it stand the way it is. She can give interviews with every newspaper in California, and it won't change the fact that there is no more money for her."

Clasping her hand, he drew her out of her chair and around the table. "There's something else you're going to have to consider, Dionne," he said, pulling her down onto his lap. "When you and I get married, it's going to cause a minor sensation."

"Married?" she gasped, shock widening her eyes.

"Surely you've heard of it," he said with amusement.

"Not from you. You never said a thing about marriage."

"I'm feeling traditional." He kissed her lightly. "I'm going to feel silly standing at the altar by myself, so I'd appreciate it if you would be there with me. The wedding photos we show our children should have both parents in them, don't you think?"

"Children?"

He nodded. "I'd like at least two, but there's room for more. I'm open to negotiation."

Behind the humor she sensed he was serious. Shock was replaced by elation, and she looped her arms around his neck. "Since you're feeling so traditional, isn't it customary for the man to ask the woman if she wants to marry him?"

He laid his forearm across her thighs to anchor her on his lap. "I can't get down on my knees at the moment."

Momentarily sobered, she murmured, "Marriage is a big step, Nick. Are you sure it's what you want?"

Unable to resist the tempting curve of her shoulder and throat, he nibbled on her scented flesh, pleased to feel her shiver. She was so responsive. Every time he touched her, she responded fully, holding nothing back.

He lifted his head. "I've never been more sure of anything in my life," he said, his voice husky with emotion.

"Why will it be a minor sensation for us to get married?"

"Modesty prohibits me from bragging extensively except to say I'm fairly well-known in my field. You're Farrell Hart's daughter with a mysterious past. Our marriage is bound to cause a stir."

She groaned. "Does it have to? I don't want our marriage to start off like some gigantic circus. Does everyone have to know?"

"We can't change who we are, Dionne. I don't want to hide our marriage as though it were something to be ashamed of. I don't care if the whole world knows I want to spend the rest of my life with you. In fact, I might insist on it."

She buried her face in his neck. She believed

him and believed in how she felt about him. She trusted him in a way she had never trusted anyone else except herself. He was the other half of her, the half that she had never known was missing until she met him.

It was the outside world she didn't trust.

Nick tightened his hold on her. He knew she wasn't comfortable with publicity in any form, even an announcement of their marriage. Under the circumstances, considering who they were, there was bound to be a write-up or two in the paper. He couldn't stop it, nor did he particularly care to. He wanted the whole world to know he was going to spend the rest of his life with Dionne.

Later, when they arrived at the estate, Nick went through every room making sure all the windows were secure while Dionne gathered up her belongings. He was putting one of her suitcases in the trunk of his Mustang when a car pulled up behind his. Up in her bedroom Dionne happened to glance out the window and saw Nick walk over to the car. Several times he looked toward the house, shaking his head. The car drove away.

When Nick returned for another suitcase, she asked, "Who was in the car?"

"Jake Trueman. He's a reporter."

She continued folding a shirt. "Oh."

"The story about Leah Buckner has caused quite a bit of interest. They want you to respond to the accusations Leah made, that you're keeping all of your father's money and giving her and his son a pittance."

"There isn't any money," she said impatiently.

Nick closed the lid of the suitcase. "I didn't know that until you told me."

She stepped over to the window. She knew what he was saying and why he was saying it. Nick wanted her to defend herself. In print. Her distaste for publicity was deep and long-standing. She didn't even like having her picture taken for her driver's license. Every segment of her father's life had been open to scrutiny, and she had been part of that until she was sixteen.

Wrapping her arms around her waist, she continued to stare out the window. "Nick, do you remember the column you wrote several years ago about shoes?"

"Vaguely. What about it?"

"You wrote about how you think people resemble shoes. Some make fashion statements, others are worn down at the heels. There are work shoes, baby shoes, pointed shoes, flat shoes, sneakers, loafers, comfortable slippers, saddle shoes. Every type of shoe for every type of person. You left out hobnail boots and the type of men who wear them. That was my father. He stomped over people as easily as breathing, leaving his footprints permanently embedded in whomever got in his way."

Nick walked slowly over to her. "And he's left a few scars on you."

She nodded. "Some of them were made in public, like the time he was cutting the ribbon for one of his new businesses and dragged me along. I had gotten braces on that morning, and was very self-conscious about them. He insisted I smile for the cameras, then laughed when he saw the braces. It had apparently slipped his mind I had the braces put on that day. The photo that appeared in the paper showed my father laughing and pointing at my mouth. It's bad enough to be embarrassed in front of a few people, worse to have the incident magnified in print."

Nick thought of the photos he had seen in the newspaper files. "Your father was responsible for those pictures in the paper, not you."

She had come to that conclusion years ago. "I know you think I should publicly defend myself, but in order to do so I would have to dredge up my father's personal life, making me no different than he was."

"Dionne, newspapers can be used for a good purpose, not just to embarrass people or for notoriety. One of the basic functions of any paper is to inform." He saw the stubborn tilt to her chin and smiled. "All right. I'll back off. I believe in the freedom of the press, but also freedom of choice. If you don't want to talk to a reporter, then I'll see they leave you alone."

She placed her hands on his chest. "You might think I'm being oversensitive about publicity, Nick, and you could be right. All I want to do is get on with my life with you. Does it really matter what other people think?"

"No, as long as what they think doesn't hurt you." Stepping back, he picked up her suitcase. "Have you got everything?"

"Did you get the old table that used to be in the kitchen? It's the only thing I want to take with me."

"It's in the trunk of your car."

"Then I guess I'm ready."

"I'll put this in your car and follow you back to the ranch. And I'll shut the front gates behind me. That way no one can get in until the new owners take possession."

During the drive to Nick's ranch Dionne took advantage of the time alone to think about what he had said. And what he hadn't said. Earlier he had warned her their marriage might cause a minor sensation. If he was right, she was either going to have to accept it or fight it. Considering he was a journalist, he might find it awkward to refuse to be interviewed in order to protect her. She had an aversion toward publicity because of the past, but Nick was her future.

He was being supportive of her feelings even when he didn't totally agree with her. If they were going to have a successful life together, she'd have to bend a little.

It wasn't until that evening she brought up something they hadn't talked about yet. With everything else that had been going on, she had pushed it to one side, but it had to be faced.

They were eating their dinner out by the pool when she said, "I'm going to have to go back to San Francisco soon, Nick."

He raised his gaze, his eyes puzzled. "Why?"

"There are a few things I have to take care of. I

have an apartment and a job waiting for me. The school has allowed me to take a leave of absence because of my father's death, but I have a contract with the school district to finish out the year."

"Can you get out of the contract?"

"I suppose I could."

He studied her carefully. "Do you want to get out of it?"

"Since it's early in the school year, the children haven't had a chance to get accustomed to me. It wouldn't be difficult for them to adjust to another teacher, but I might be leaving the school in a difficult position if they can't find a permanent replacement."

He shrugged and speared a bite of steak. "It's not a problem. We'll stay at your apartment and come back here on school holidays. Next year you could apply for a teaching job here."

She gaped at him. It was the last thing she had expected him to say. "You would move to San Francisco?"

"Of course. Our marriage is going to be a partnership, not a dictatorship. If you want to teach in San Francisco this year, that's all right with me. After you finish your contract, we can move back here permanently."

"You have your work and the ranch, Nick. I couldn't ask you to give up everything and move to San Francisco."

He hated the thought that kept running through his mind, that she might not come back. As sure as he was of his own feelings, he wasn't entirely sure of her. There was no way she was going to San Francisco without him.

"If you can give me several days, I'll make arrangements for someone to feed and exercise the horses. I can write my column in your apartment."

She leaned forward and placed her hand over his. "I couldn't ask you to do that, Nick. To give up everything you have here for eight months."

He grasped her fingers. "You aren't asking me. And it's not forever. We can spend weekends and holidays here. We'll be together. That's what's important, not where we'll live."

She shook her head in wonderment. "You're an exceptional man, Nicholas Lyon."

He smiled broadly. "That's true."

The following morning Dionne made a couple of phone calls to San Francisco, one to the principal of her school and one to her neighbor who had been watering her plants. Mr. Trafalgar was pleased she would be coming back to teach and Mrs. Resort would be happy to air out the apartment and get in food supplies for her.

That afternoon Nick drove into Carmel to ask Marty to horse-sit. It required a little explaining after Marty asked Nick if he had lost his mind. Finally Nick persuaded his friend that he knew exactly what he was doing, and Marty agreed to take care of the livestock when Nick wasn't there. Nick had meant what he had told Dionne. Nothing was as important as their being together.

The following day, while Nick was in town ordering supplies for the ranch to last during their absence, Dionne received an unexpected phone call from Marty. When she told him Nick wasn't there, Marty said he knew that. He didn't want to talk to Nick. He wanted to talk to her. Could she meet him somewhere in town without Nick knowing about it? he asked. Puzzled, she agreed. Marty named a place, giving her directions.

Fortunately Nick hadn't returned by the time she had changed clothes, so it wasn't necessary for her to make excuses to go into Carmel. She found the restaurant with little trouble and was shown to Marty's table. Nick's friend stood up as she approached, extending his hand.

She refused anything to eat, settling for a cup of coffee. "Why did you want to meet me without Nick knowing, Mr. Lawson?"

"Marty, please. I know this is a little unusual, but I thought it would be a good idea if we had a talk. Nick told me yesterday about going to San Francisco with you."

Since he had gotten right to the point, she decided she would too. "Do you think he's making a mistake?"

Shaking his head, Marty smiled. "I've been Nick's friend a long time, Dionne. That doesn't mean I feel I have the right to make judgments about his life. I've never seen him as enthusiastic or as happy as he looked yesterday when he told me he was getting married. I haven't asked to meet you today because I'm going to make any objections."

"Then why did you want to see me alone?"

Unusually hesitant, Marty pursed his lips for a moment before going on. "When I said I would give him one of the best farewell parties on the Peninsula, he told me to forget it." Leaning forward, Marty rested his arms on the table. "Now this is a man who has always enjoyed getting together with his friends, and believe me, he's got a lot of friends here. He wouldn't explain why all of a sudden he's not interested in having a party with his friends, especially one in his honor."

Dionne looked down at the table. She had the sinking feeling she knew why. Just to make sure, she asked, "Are most of his friends people connected with the local newspaper?"

Marty frowned. "Some of them are. Why?"

"I'm afraid I'm the reason he doesn't want a farewell party." In a few succinct sentences she explained her aversion to publicity. "Nick knows how I feel."

"Ah-ha," Marty said softly, finally comprehending what the problem was.

Dionne nodded. "Why don't you ask the waitress to bring us each a refill? There are a couple of things I want to discuss with you."

Nick was walking out of the barn when Dionne parked in front of the ranch house. After waving to him, she stepped around to the trunk and began taking out several packages.

"Good Lord, Dionne," he said when he joined her. "Did you buy out the stores?"

She handed him three bags. "I just got a few things I needed before we leave."

He followed her toward the house. "It's going to be fun trying to pack all of this into the car with what we've already packed. Don't they have stores in San Francisco?"

Opening the door for him, she said casually, "I wanted something special to wear tomorrow night. And I needed a few other things. Just put them down on the couch for now."

"What's happening tomorrow night?"

When his arms were empty, she walked into them. "I thought since it was going to be our last night here, we should go out for dinner. What do you think?"

With her body pressed against his, he found it difficult to think at all. "If that's what you want to do, fine. We'll go out. Do you have anywhere in mind?"

She nodded. "As a matter of fact, I do. Canaveri's."

Nick approved of Dionne's shopping spree after she came out of the bedroom. The black sheath dress flowed over her curves, thin straps leaving her shoulders bare. The Spanish shawl he had seen at her father's house was draped over her arm.

He had second thoughts about taking her anywhere except the bedroom, but she was already walking toward the door.

When they reached Canaveri's, so many cars

were parked on the side street, Nick had to park a block away.

"Maybe I should have made reservations," he said as they strolled toward the restaurant. "It looks like Canaveri's is busy tonight."

Dionne slipped her hand through the crook of his arm. "I'm sure Momma will squeeze us in somewhere."

When Nick opened the door, he squinted his eyes to peer inside. At first he wondered if the Canaveris had decided to economize on their electricity bill. The restaurant was surprisingly dark, with only a few lighted candles on tables.

As soon as he stepped inside, lights flooded the room and dozens of people yelled, "Surprise!"

Astounded, he looked around, seeing familiar faces. Momma, Papa, Marty, Barry, some reporters from the paper, and other friends. Cameras flashed one right after the other, capturing his surprised expression—and the woman standing beside him.

He jerked his head around to look at Dionne. She was smiling. When another flash went off, he saw her flinch, but her smile remained.

He took her hand. "Did you know about this?"

She nodded, then let out a soft exclamation as Marty grabbed her and hugged her. Keeping one arm around her, he turned to Nick. "You've got quite a lady here, Nick. She's underhanded and sneaky. I like her."

Nick held Dionne's gaze. "You planned this?"

"With Marty's help. He's been calling people the past two days."

Nick didn't have time to digest the fact that Dionne had been responsible for gathering his friends all together. The other guests had surrounded them, and he was pulled into the restaurant and the throng of people. The three-piece band began to play, adding to the festivities. Keeping a tight grip on Dionne's hand, he tried to introduce her to as many people as he could.

Not only was the party itself a surprise, Nick was astonished by Dionne's participation, considering the place was packed with newspaper people. She chatted freely with Barry, knowing full well he was the editor in chief of the local paper. Nick was probably the only one who noticed her turning away whenever she saw a camera pointed in her direction. It was a subtle evasion and possibly automatic on her part.

When Momma managed to get the two of them together, she asked in her boisterous voice, "So when's the wedding?"

"We haven't had a chance to talk about it yet," Dionne said.

That led to a variety of suggestions, from Christmas to Valentine's Day. Nick made his own to Dionne when they had a rare few moments alone. "They aren't going to be satisfied until we give them a date. You realize everyone is expecting us to get married here, not in San Francisco."

"My first school holiday is Thanksgiving. We could come back to the ranch and get married then. Your mother should be here by then."

As far as he was concerned, they were already

married in every way except legally. He agreed
with Thanksgiving and everyone cheered when he
announced the date.

It was late when they finally left the restaurant.
Actually it was early in the morning when Nick
unlocked his front door. Once inside he shed his
jacket and loosened his tie. Dionne leaned against
the door, letting the shawl slide off her.

She kicked off her heels and hobbled toward
the couch, dragging the shawl behind her. "I know
Marty is your best friend, Nick, but the man can-
not dance. I swear he stepped on my feet a dozen
times while we were dancing."

Instead of being amused, Nick closed the distance between them and stood in front of her. His
expression was serious, his eyes dark with an
unnamed emotion. "I don't want to talk about
Marty. I want to discuss the party, the reason you
had for giving it."

She had been expecting him to ask that question all night long. "Marty said you liked parties
but had turned down his offer for a farewell party.
I was the reason you didn't want to get together
with your friends because some of them are
newspapermen and women. I couldn't let you sacrifice your friends for me, Nick. You're already
giving up your life here at the ranch, if only tem-
porarily. That isn't fair."

He raised his hands to her shoulders, enjoying
the feel of her silky bare skin. "It's not a sacrifice,
Dionne. You're more important to me than breathing."

He was a man who made his living with words, she knew, but he also deserved to hear them from her.

"Everything has happened so fast," she said, "yet so slowly. Meeting you, falling in love with you, was like a flash of sunlight piercing a dark cloud. Yet my father's affairs seemed to drag on forever. What I thought was so important before no longer mattered. I finally realized what truly is important." Her voice caught as she continued. "*You* are important. What we've found together is important. For a fairly intelligent school teacher, I've been remarkably stupid in sorting out the past and the present. I've finally put the past where it belongs, Nick. Now I have plenty of room for a future."

His fingers eased under the straps of her dress, sliding them off her shoulders. "All I want," he said softly, "is for us to be together, to make you as happy as you make me."

She cupped his face in her hands. "Nick, I've never been happier than I have been with you. I plan on being ecstatically happy the rest of my life. Even when we have disagreements."

"I would rather make love with you than fight with you," he murmured as he slowly lowered her dress, exposing the gentle curve of her breasts.

She smiled. "That comes after the fight. It's called making up."

"We could pretend we just had a fight so we can make up now."

Her fingers worked at the knot of his tie. "I'm marrying a very brilliant man."

"I'm glad you realize that."

"You've given me so much, Nick," she said seriously. "I wanted to give you something too."

He stroked her face. "You've given me yourself and your love. Those are the greatest gifts a man could ever ask for or need."

Her smile changed, becoming soft and sensual. She backed up a step. Holding out her hand, she took another step backward in the direction of his bedroom.

"I have another gift for you."

His gaze focused on her moist mouth, then dropped to her breasts. "Do you?"

Her fingers curled around his hand. "It's in the bedroom."

"Do I get to unwrap it?" he asked, walking forward.

Instead of moving back as he had expected, she stepped toward him, bringing her soft frame against his. "Please."

THE EDITOR'S CORNER

Next month you have even more wonderful reading to look forward to from LOVESWEPT. We're publishing another four of our most-asked-for books as Silver Signature Editions, which as you know are some of the best romances from our early days! In this group you'll find **ONCE IN A BLUE MOON** (#26) by Billie Green, **SEND NO FLOWERS** (#51) by Sandra Brown, and two interrelated books—**CAPTURE THE RAINBOW** and **TOUCH THE HORIZON** by Iris Johansen. Those of you who haven't had the pleasure of savoring these scrumptious stories are in for one bountiful feast! But do leave room on your reading menu for our six new LOVESWEPTs, because they, too, are gourmet delights!

A new Iris Johansen book is always something to celebrate, and Iris provides you with a real gem next month. **TENDER SAVAGE,** LOVESWEPT #420, is the love story of charismatic revolutionary leader Ricardo Lazaro and daring Lara Clavel. Determined to free the man who saved her brother's life, Lara risks her own life in a desperate plan that takes a passionate turn. Trapped with Ricardo in his cramped jail cell, Lara intends to playact a seduction to fool their jailer—but instead she discovers a savage need to be possessed, body and soul, by her freedom fighter. Lara knew she was putting herself in jeopardy, but she didn't expect the worst danger to be her overwhelming feelings for the rebel leader of the Caribbean island. Iris is a master at developing tension between strong characters, and placing them in a cell together is one sure way to ignite those incendiary sparks. Enjoy **TENDER SAVAGE,** it's vintage Johansen.

Every so often a new writer comes along whose work seems custom-made for LOVESWEPT. We feel Patricia Burroughs is such a writer. Patricia's first LOVESWEPT is **SOME ENCHANTED SEASON,** #421, and in it she offers readers the very best of what you've come to expect in our romances—humor, tender emotion, sparkling dialogue, smoldering sensuality, carefully crafted prose, and characters who tug at your heart. When artist Kevyn Llewellyn spots the man who is the epitome of the warrior-god she has to paint, she can't believe her good fortune. But convincing him to pose for her is another story. Rusty Rivers thinks the lady with the silver-streaked hair is a kook, but he's irresistibly drawn to her nonetheless. An incredible tease, Rusty tells her she can use his body only if he can use hers! Kevyn can't

(continued)

deal with his steamy embraces and fiery kisses, she's always felt so isolated and alone. The last thing she wants in her life is a hunk with a wicked grin. But, of course, Rusty is too much a hero to take no for an answer! This story is appealing on so many levels, you'll be captivated from page one.

If Janet Evanovich weren't such a dedicated writer, I think she could have had a meteoric career as a comedienne. Her books make me laugh until I cry, and **WIFE FOR HIRE, LOVESWEPT #422**, is no exception. Hero Hank Mallone spotted trouble when Maggie Toone sat down and said she'd marry him. But Hank isn't one to run from a challenge, and having Maggie pretend to be his wife in order to improve his reputation seemed like the challenge of a lifetime. His only problem comes when he starts to falling in love with the tempting firecracker of a woman. Maggie never expected her employer to be drop-dead handsome or to be the image of every fantasy she'd ever had. Cupid really turns the tables on these two, and you won't want to miss a single minute of the fun!

Another wonderful writer makes her LOVESWEPT debut this month, and she fits into our lineup with grace and ease. Erica Spindler is a talented lady who has published several books for Silhouette under her own name. Her first LOVESWEPT, #423, is a charmingly fresh story called **RHYME OR REASON**. Heroine Alex Clare is a dreamer with eyes that sparkle like the crystal she wears as a talisman, and Dr. Walker Chadwick Ridgeman thinks he needs to have his head examined for being drawn to the lovely seductress. After all, he's a serious man who believes in what he can see, and Alex believes the most important things in life are those that you can't see or touch but only feel. Caught up in her sensual spell, Walker learns firsthand of the changes a magical love can bring about.

Judy Gill's next three books aren't part of a "series," but they will feature characters whose paths will cross. In **DREAM MAN, LOVESWEPT #424**, heroine Jeanie Leslie first meets Max McKenzie in her dreams. She'd conjured up the dashingly handsome hero as the answer to all her troubled sister's needs. But when he actually walks into her office one day in response to the intriguing ad she'd run, Jeanie knows without a doubt that she could never fix him up with her sister—because she wants him for herself! Max applies for the "Man Wanted" position out of curiosity, but once he sets eyes on Jeanie, he's suddenly compelled to convince

(continued)

her how right they are for each other. While previously neither would admit to wanting a permanent relationship, after they meet they can't seem to think about anything else. But it takes a brush with death to bring these two passionate lovers together forever!

Helen Mittermeyer closes the month with **FROZEN IDOL**, LOVESWEPT #425, the final book in her *Men of Ice* trilogy. If her title doesn't do it, her story will send a thrill down your spine over the romance between untouchable superstar Dolph Wakefield and smart and sexy businesswoman Bedelia Fronsby. Fate intervenes in Dolph's life when Bedelia shows up ten years after she'd vanished without a trace and left him to deal with the deepest feelings he'd ever had for a woman. Now the owner of a company that plans to finance Dolph's next film, Bedelia finds herself succumbing once again to the impossible Viking of a man whose power over her emotions has only strengthened with time. When Dolph learns the true reason she'd left him, he can't help but decide to cherish her always. Once again Helen delivers a story fans are sure to love!

In the upcoming months we will begin several unique promotions which we're certain will be hits with readers. Starting in October and continuing through January, you will be able to accumulate coupons from the backs of our books which you may redeem for special hardcover "Keepsake Editions" of LOVESWEPTs by your favorite authors. Watch for more information on how to save your coupons and where to send them.

Another innovative new feature we're planning to offer is a "900" number readers can use to reach LOVESWEPT by telephone. As soon as the line is set up, we'll let you know the number—until then, keep reading!

Sincerely,

Susann Brailey

Susann Brailey
Editor
LOVESWEPT
Bantam Books
666 Fifth Avenue
New York, NY 10103

FAN OF THE MONTH

Carollyn McCauley

After seeing the Fan of the Month in the backs of LOVESWEPTs, I wished that I'd have a chance to be one. I thought it would never happen. Due to a close friend and the people at LOVESWEPT, I got my wish granted.

I've been a reader of romance novels for twenty years, ever since I finished nursing school.

LOVESWEPTs arrive at the Waldenbooks store I go to around the first week of the month. Starting that week I haunt the store until the LOVESWEPTs are placed on the shelves, then, within two or three days, I've finished reading them and have to wait anxiously for the next month's shipment.

I have a few favorite authors: Iris Johansen, Kay Hooper, Billie Green, Sharon and Tom Curtis, and many more. As far as I'm concerned, the authors that LOVESWEPT chooses are the cream of the crop in romance. I encourage the readers of LOVESWEPT who buy books only by authors they've read before to let themselves go and take a chance on the new authors. They'll find they'll be pleasantly surprised and will never be disappointed. The books are well written, and the unusual and unique plots will capture their attention. From the first book in the line to the current ones, they have all held my attention from page one to the last, causing me to experience a variety of emotions and feelings.

Over the years of reading the different romances available, I've cut back on the amount I purchase due to the cost. LOVESWEPT has maintained such a high standard of quality that I'll always buy all six each month!

OFFICIAL RULES TO
LOVESWEPT'S
DREAM MAKER GIVEAWAY
(See entry card in center of this book)

1. NO PURCHASE NECESSARY. To enter both the sweepstakes and accept the risk-free trial offer, follow the directions published on the insert card in this book. Return your entry on the reply card provided. If you do not wish to take advantage of the risk-free trial offer, but wish to enter the sweepstakes, return the entry card only with the "FREE ENTRY" sticker attached, or send your name and address on a 3x5 card to : Loveswept Sweepstakes, Bantam Books, PO Box 985, Hicksville, NY 11802-9827.

2. To be eligible for the prizes offered, your entry must be received by September 17, 1990. We are not responsible for late, lost or misdirected mail. Winners will be selected on or about October 16, 1990 in a random drawing under the supervision of Marden Kane, Inc., an independent judging organization, and except for those prizes which will be awarded to the first 50 entrants, prizes will be awarded after that date. By entering this sweepstakes, each entrant accepts and agrees to be bound by these rules and the decision of the judges which shall be final and binding. This sweepstakes will be presented in conjunction with various book offers sponsored by Bantam Books under the following titles: Agatha Christie "Mystery Showcase", Louis L'Amour "Great American Getaway", Loveswept "Dreams Can Come True" and Loveswept "Dream Makers". Although the prize options and graphics of this Bantam Books sweepstakes will vary in each of these book offers, the value of each prize level will be approximately the same and prize winners will have the options of selecting any prize offered within the prize level won.

3. Prizes in the Loveswept "Dream Maker" sweepstakes: Grand Prize (1) 14 Day trip to either Hawaii, Europe or the Caribbean. Trip includes round trip air transportation from any major airport in the US and hotel accomodations (approximate retail value $6,000); Bonus Prize (1) $1,000 cash in addition to the trip; Second Prize (1) 27" Color TV (approximate retail value $900).

4. This sweepstakes is open to residents of the US, and Canada (excluding the province of Quebec), who are 18 years of age or older. Employees of Bantam Books, Bantam Doubleday Dell Publishing Group Inc., their affiliates and subsidiaries, Marden Kane Inc. and all other agencies and persons connected with conducting this sweepstakes and their immediate family members are not eligible to enter this sweepstakes. This offer is subject to all applicable laws and regulations and is void in the province of Quebec and wherever prohibited or restricted by law. In order to win a prize, residents of Canada will be required to correctly answer a time-limited arithmetical skill-testing question.

5. Winners will be notified by mail and will be required to execute an affidavit of eligibility and release which must be returned within 14 days of notification or an alternate winner will be selected. Prizes are not transferable. Trip prize must be taken within one year of notification and is subject to airline departure schedules and ticket and accommodation availability. Winner must have a valid passport. No substitution will be made for any prize except as offered. If a prize should be unavailable at sweepstakes end, sponsor reserves the right to substitute a prize of equal or greater value. Winners agree that the sponsor, its affiliates, and their agencies and employees shall not be liable for injury, loss or damage of any kind resulting from an entrant's participation in this offer or from the acceptance or use of the prizes awarded. Odds of winning are dependant upon the number of entries received. Taxes, if any, are the sole responsibility of the winners. Winner's entry and acceptance of any prize offered constitutes permission to use the winner's name, photograph or other likeness for purposes of advertising and promotion on behalf of Bantam Books and Bantam Doubleday Dell Publishing Group Inc. without additional compensation to the winner.

6. For a list of winners (available after 10/16/90), send a self addressed stamped envelope to Bantam Books Winners List, PO Box 704, Sayreville, NJ 08871.

7. The free gifts are available only to entrants who also agree to sample the Loveswept subscription program on the terms described. The sweepstakes prizes offered by affixing the "Free Entry" sticker to the Entry Form are available to all entrants, whether or not an entrant chooses to affix the "Free Books" sticker to the Entry Form.